# The Ultimate Christmas Gift

*Best friends, a surrogate baby,*
*and a chance for love…*

Best friends Emma Hayes and Abbie Cook will do *anything* for each other. So when nurse Abbie asks Emma if she'll be her surrogate and carry the baby she longs for, of course she doesn't refuse.

But as Christmas comes it's not just the new baby that turns their lives upside down. Because for both women there's a chance for love…if they're only brave enough to take it!

Read Abbie and Callum's story in

*The Nurse's Special Delivery*

And discover Emma and Nixon's story in

*Her New Year Baby Surprise*

Both available now!

Dear Reader,

A woman having a baby for someone else has to be one of the most unselfish gifts she can ever give. I know people who have children from surrogate mothers and how this has changed their lives in a very positive way. This has always been a story I've wanted to write, and when better than in a duet with the wonderful Louisa George?

Emma Hayes is a solo mother with a big heart, and when her best friend cannot carry her pregnancies to full term it is only natural for her to offer to have Abbie's baby.

It is this generosity and kindness and her courage that has Dr Nixon Wright sitting up and taking notice of Emma as more than a nurse and casual friend. But while his heart is leading him into love, his history is hauling on the brakes and trying to keep him safe and single. Of course his heart's going to win, but Emma won't make it easy for him. If she's going to love him back she wants the whole deal—not just the pieces Nixon offers.

I hope you enjoy reading this story to find out how Nixon wins over Emma as much as I enjoyed writing it.

Cheers!

*Sue MacKay*

sue.mackay56@yahoo.com

# HER NEW YEAR BABY SURPRISE

BY

SUE MACKAY

Published in Great Britain 2017
By Mills & Boon, an imprint of HarperCollins*Publishers*
1 London Bridge Street, London, SE1 9GF



ISBN: 978-0-263-92682-8

Our policy is to use papers that are natural, renewable and recyclable products and made from wood grown in sustainable forests. The logging and manufacturing processes conform to the legal environmental regulations of the country of origin.

Printed and bound in Spain
by CPI, Barcelona

**Sue MacKay** lives with her husband in New Zealand's beautiful Marlborough Sounds, with the water on her doorstep and the birds and the trees at her back door. It is the perfect setting to indulge her passions of entertaining friends by cooking them sumptuous meals, drinking fabulous wine, going for hill walks or kayaking around the bay—and, of course, writing stories.

**Books by Sue MacKay**

**Mills & Boon Medical Romance**

*Reunited...in Paris!*
*A December to Remember*
*Breaking All Their Rules*
*Dr White's Baby Wish*
*The Army Doc's Baby Bombshell*
*Resisting Her Army Doc Rival*
*Pregnant with the Boss's Baby*
*Falling for Her Fake Fiancé*

Visit the Author Profile page
at millsandboon.co.uk for more titles.

To my duet partner and wonderful writing friend,
Louisa George.

Loved writing a duet with you again.

Hugs, Sue.

**Praise for**
**Sue MacKay**

'I highly recommend this story to all lovers of romance: it is moving, emotional, a joy to read!'

—*Goodreads* on
*A December to Remember*

# CHAPTER ONE

'JUST LOVE HER, OKAY?' Emma Hayes told her best friend as exhaustion from giving birth ripped through her aching, painful body and threatened to tip her into sleep. Sleep, where she could hide for a while. Then she'd wake up and still have to face up to the fact she'd had Abbie's baby for her and now her own arms were empty.

Abbie didn't raise her eyes from the precious bundle she held against her breast as she replied, 'I already do. I'm besotted. Completely. And I love you with all my heart.'

Aww, sniff. More damned tears. 'I know you do.' There'd never been any doubt. Love had been why she'd done this crazy, amazing, scary thing in the first place. 'This wouldn't have happened if you didn't, and if I didn't reciprocate those feelings.'

Sitting carefully on the edge of the bed, Abbie leaned into Emma, mindful of the baby cradled between them. 'I can't describe my feelings. All the waiting and hoping and now here she is.' She brushed a kiss over Em's wet cheek. 'Thank you so much. Again.'

Emma lightly wound her arms around her friend and their precious bundle. 'Stop saying that, okay?' She didn't want gratitude; she didn't need to be thanked. That they'd come through the pregnancy without an argument said a lot for their friendship, but then, it'd been strong since the day they met at Queenstown Primary more than twenty years ago. But at the moment, the only thing she knew for certain was a few minutes to herself were imperative if she was to keep her equilibrium now that she'd given birth. 'Go be a mum while I get some shut-eye.'

She needed to fall into the haze filling her head to forget the pain of the birth and remember only the relief that everything had gone well, despite the baby arriving early. Happiness and sadness wound together in her heart at the wonder in Abbie's eyes as she gazed down on the tiny, beautiful little girl tucked into a pink hospital blanket. A child who'd never know her father; who had been created through artificial insemination.

One of the two most beautiful girls in the world. Emma's heart swelled with love and longing. 'Rosie.' Suddenly, more than anything in the world, Emma needed to hold her own daughter. Her other daughter, barely five and full of energy and mischief.

*No! Don't go there. Grace is Abbie's. Always has been, always will be.*

Snatching up the phone, she texted her mother.

It's over. Baby's gorgeous. Please bring Rosie to me.Xx

Abbie looked up, her eyes filled with awe and trepidation. 'This is for real, isn't it? This is where I get to step up to the mark and be a mum in all ways possible except carrying her myself.' Tears streamed down Abbie's cheeks. 'This is why you gave me such a precious gift. To be a mother.' Her voice trailed off in a whisper, the last words barely audible.

'Isn't it the best?' Emma whispered back around a lump in her throat and a dash of emptiness. But not one regret. Abbie deserved good things. If there'd been a moment when being the mummy tummy might've been difficult,

Emma suspected it would've been minutes ago when the midwife had handed Abbie the baby, not her. But no. She'd been fine about it, hadn't had a sudden change of heart, so she now reiterated, 'Grace has been yours since conception.' Abbie's and Michael's, though he would never get to see his daughter, never hold her or know her. His only role in the pregnancy had been to leave sperm in the bank for this very day.

Emma bit down on a soft smile.

*I did the right thing by them.*

Abbie and Michael had stood by her through the hideous, violent days of her marriage as much as her family had. They'd helped pick up the scattered pieces of her dreams afterwards, had shown with their own strong love for each other that she could make a life with Rosie without looking back. That they could be a family without a man in her life. Not that she'd ever been in the market for a new husband. No, thank you very much. Been there, had the bruises and fractures to show for it.

Her friends had also made sure she and Rosie never went without fun and laughter. This had been her way of returning the love. Knowing the baby would be living next door in the adjoining apartment would make everything easier to come to terms with. Abbie was not rushing out of Queenstown to some place else in New Zealand to keep her daughter to herself. Though who knew where she might end up if the Scotsman pulled his head out of his backside and found he couldn't live without Abbie. Right now, she wanted to throttle him for hurting Abbie with his uncertainties.

They'd always been there for each other on the days when Rosie wouldn't stop crying and Emma needed a break, or other days where Abbie couldn't cope with losing Michael. Their friendship was solid, and it would take a hurricane of massive proportions to break it. Today, with a baby and a broken heart to deal with, Abbie needed her support more than ever.

'If only I had that with a man.'

'Had what?' Abbie asked without taking her eyes off Grace.

'The same trust and sharing and loving and laughs—and tears—you had with Michael.'

Abbie's head shot up, surprise widening her eyes. 'That's a shift in your thinking.'

'Told you I needed sleep. Must be baby brain.' She did not want a man in her life. The only man she'd loved unreservedly had developed a pair of fast and hard fists along with a cruel mouth. She wasn't going to repeat that experience in an attempt to find love. Only the unwise didn't learn from their mistakes, and Alvin had been a *mistake*. Definitely better off without a man in her life, and the reason she turned down any—the few—date invitations. Her body was safe, and, more importantly, Rosie was protected. There was already plenty of love in her life—Rosie, Abbie, and her fiercely protective brothers and father, and her ever patient mother. Who needed someone special when she was surrounded by those guys? Talk about greedy. Not everyone got so lucky.

'Any man in particular causing this left-field idea? An emergency specialist by any chance?' asked her cheeky friend.

'Nixon and I get on fine as friends. I turned him down for a date once.'

'You never told me.' Abbie eyeballed her, then grinned. 'Mr Cool isn't as uninvolved as he'd like you to think.'

Sigh. 'Yeah, right. I had enough going on with the pregnancy and Rosie. I didn't need complications with a man.'

Abbie smiled sadly. 'Guess I can't argue with that today considering Cal has just dumped me.'

*Ping!*

Saved by the phone.

Nearly there. Princess couldn't wait any longer. Mum. Xxx

Then the baby—

*Grace, Emma, her name is Grace.*

The baby gave a small cry and Emma's breasts tightened painfully. Breasts that did not have a role to play in feeding this gorgeous infant.

Abbie looked up, panic in her eyes. 'What now?'

'You feed her. Food, warmth, love.' Under the blanket, Emma's hands clenched against the urge to reach for the baby to place her on her breast. No surprise here. Her body didn't understand it was no longer the mother, despite the repeated messages from her brain. All it heard were the calls from her heart.

The midwife bustled into the room. 'Did I hear Baby cry? She'll be wanting to be fed.' Her eyes flicked to Emma, and she gave an almost imperceptible lopsided nod as if to ask, *How are you doing?*

Emma nodded back. Okay, she mouthed.

*But take them away so my breasts can settle down.*

'She's making noises like she's hungry,' Abbie muttered, still gazing at the baby, only now with trepidation.

'You'll be fine, Abbie.' The midwife had all the reassuring words and actions. The baby hadn't latched on when first placed against her mother's breast, but hopefully now she would. 'We'll go along to the nursery and I'll start you learning to breastfeed. Emma needs to rest.' She helped Abbie to her feet.

'Right.' Abbie held Grace as though afraid of dropping her as she moved out of the room. With her injured arm, it was a distinct possibility, so it was no wonder she held her daughter carefully.

Emma's eyes tracked her until she disappeared around

the corner, a lump the size of Lake Wakatipu in her throat and her chest painfully tight. Abbie and Grace. Her friend and her daughter. Her daughter? Or Abbie's? Definitely Abbie's. But…

No buts.

*Where's Rosie?*

A fierce ache throbbed in her breasts and there was nothing she could do to appease it. Bizarre didn't begin to describe the fact that Abbie was able to breastfeed her daughter. 'The wonder of modern-day drugs.' Emma carefully slid further down the bed. The irony being that she would need something to help with stopping her milk supply, or at least to dull the pain while nature ran its course. Uncomfortable days were ahead, then hopefully everything would settle down and she'd get back to life as she knew it—raising Rosie and working day shifts in the emergency department downstairs; saving for a deposit on a house and keeping her head below the radar when it came to men.

'Mummy, where's the baby? Can I hold it?' Rosie raced into the room, staring all about. 'I can't see the baby.' She leapt onto the bed and lifted the cover to peer underneath.

Emma gasped at the sudden movement. 'Easy. Mummy's sore.'

'Where is it?'

'It's a little girl and her name is Grace, darling. She's gone to the nursery with Abbie,' Emma explained and had to bite down on the chuckle brought on by her daughter's disappointment.

'But I want to hold her.'

At least she wasn't jealous. The midwife had warned that Rosie could initially be anti the baby, might see her as competition for her mother's affections. But these were unusual circumstances.

'Rosie, love, remember what I told you?' Emma's

mother appeared in the doorway. 'The baby will be tired and only Abbie can hold her just now. You'll get a turn soon.'

Really? Would Rosie go along with having to wait? Emma raised an eyebrow at her mother. They were good at talking like this around a certain little madam.

A nod. A frown. An eloquent shrug. Then in real speak, 'I've been fobbing off demands to come see you since I picked her up. Daniel got tied up with a client and couldn't make it,' she explained. 'When I received your text we were already pulling into the car park, the word "no" having long gone out the window. She was far more interested in the baby than what happened at school.'

'That's saying something.' Emma laughed. Rosie believed school had been created just for her.

'Where's the nursy?' Rosie bounced up and down on the bed.

'Nursery,' Emma corrected automatically as she tensed against the sharp pain brought on by the bed turning into Rosie's trampoline. 'Can you sit still, love?'

'What's the nursy?' The bounces reduced in severity but didn't stop.

'Nursery. It's where the babies sleep while they're in the hospital.' In this case anyway. Emma reached for her girl. 'Got a hug for Mummy?'

Little arms wound tightly around her neck. 'A big, big, big one, Mummy.' And a sloppy kiss apparently.

Not to mention the elbow in her belly. Carefully dislodging Rosie's arm, she kissed her daughter's forehead. 'Thank you, darling.'

'Do you like my hug, Mummy? It's special for you.'

Tears sprang into Emma's eyes, and she tightened her hold on her daughter. Pressing her face into the abundant dark curls, she sniffed and croaked, 'It's the best hug ever.'

It really, really was, and she might need plenty of them over the coming days.

'How are you, sweetheart?' Her mum kissed her gently on the other cheek and passed over a handful of tissues.

'I'm good. About everything. Though I feel like a freight truck's driven through me.'

There was doubt in those knowledgeable eyes that she'd known all her life. Not even shock tactics had diverted her mum from her real mission. 'When do you see the psychologist?'

*Give me strength.*

That was the last person she wanted to talk to, but there'd be no avoiding that particular conversation. It was part of the surrogacy deal she'd signed that she talk to everyone this side of the Crown Ranges about her feelings. If the shrink lady didn't come looking for her then her mother would be hauling her to the counsellor's rooms herself.

'In a couple of days, unless I need her sooner. Honestly, Mum, I'm fine. When Grace cried, I felt a tug on the heartstrings, but she has always been Abbie's baby and nothing's changed.'

*Nothing I can't handle. I hope.*

Hell, what if she couldn't manage, was crippled with longing for the baby that wasn't hers?

Her mum cut through the sudden pain in her head. 'If you're sure.'

'I am,' she answered more forcefully than she intended. Pushing the demons back into their box? 'At the moment I'm more in need of sleep.'

Her mother smiled her special mum smile and gently pushed the hair away from Emma's forehead. 'I'm proud of you. I don't think I could've done what you have.'

More tears. 'Thanks, Mum. You got a hug for me too?' Why did she need so many?

Rosie squirmed in close, pushing her way under Emma's right arm. 'Me, too, Mummy. I love hugs, don't I?'

'This a hug fest?' The booming question came from across the room.

Emma's eyes flew open. Nixon stood at the entrance, looking uncertain of his welcome. 'Hey. You want to join in?'

'Me? I don't think so. There's a crowd already.'

'Chicken.' The challenge slipped out with no input from her brain. No problem, he'd refuse. He'd asked her out about six months ago. With every other available female, and some not so available, swooning at his feet, she knew she'd shocked him by saying no. She wanted nothing more to do with dating men, or so she'd told herself over and over since that day, trying not to wonder what it would've been like going out with Nixon. Once he learned she was pregnant, he'd got over his shock quick smart and they'd started getting on great guns as friends. Perfect. Really? Was it perfect?

A wriggle, a squirm, and Rosie shrieked, 'Nixon, have you seen the baby? Mummy won't take me to see it and I want to hold her.'

Emma's mother stepped back, rubbing her ear. 'Quieter, Rosie.'

Emma ran her hand over Rosie's curls. 'That's not what I said. Abbie's feeding Grace so you have to be patient.'

'That's like asking a cat to ignore the mouse running across its paws.' Nixon winked. 'Especially with this one.' He knew Rosie from the times she used to be dropped off at the department after pre-school on the days Emma was running late signing off. Her daughter had fallen under his spell in the flash of a chocolate bar and a wide smile. Easily bribed, her girl.

Nixon moved up, leaned over and wrapped his arms

around Emma. 'You're looking good for what you've been through.'

A warm sigh trickled across her lips. This hug felt special. The perfect elixir for lurking emotions left over from handing the baby to Abbie. Emma leaned forward ever so slightly to rest against Nixon's chest and breathed deeply, absorbing the man scent and strength. She lurched backwards. This was all wrong. They were pals, not lovers.

There had been one time she'd said too much to him. At the end of a particularly hectic shift she'd been tired and achy, heavily pregnant and despondent, and when he'd walked out of the department with her and suggested a wind-down drink over the road at the café, she'd burst into tears. It had to have been the tea that loosened her tongue, or otherwise why had she spilled her guts to Nixon about her feelings over giving up the baby? The feelings she wouldn't share with Abbie so as not to rattle her friend's confidence that she would hand over Abbie's baby.

He'd listened without interruption as she'd explained her fear of not being able to let go the baby, which would break her friend's heart along with her own. Not once did Nixon say it was her fault she was in that predicament. He'd shown another side to himself. He'd always been popular, but also somewhat wary, and known to be a focused, caring doctor. She doubted anyone at work had seen Nixon so thoughtful and considerate about something unrelated to work. Which made her wonder what else he was hiding behind his everyday face. And glad she'd turned him down for that date. She had enough of her own problems to be carrying on with, without taking on anyone else's.

Now he stepped back, those thoughtful eyes watching her too closely for comfort.

'Mum, you haven't met Nixon, have you? Nixon Wright, this is my mum Kathy Hayes. Nixon's our emergency specialist,' she added for clarity. No point raising her mother's hopes that she'd found a man. How her mother could want her to get married again was beyond Emma. Not after her last fiasco. But then, all her family held onto some guilt over that. They'd fallen under Alvin's spell too and had encouraged her marriage.

'You're not a local.' Her mother shook Nixon's hand, appraising the tall, strapping specimen before her as if she was about to interview him. Which, being her mother, was definitely on the cards. And her mum had nothing on her brothers or father. Emma wouldn't put it past them to tie any man she might be interested in up to the fence and throw icy water over him while proceeding with an interrogation about whether he knew his hands were not made to be used against their sister and daughter.

He gave a light smile. 'I shifted here from Dunedin a year ago, so, no, most people don't know what I like to eat for breakfast or what grades I got in school.'

There were few secrets in Queenstown amongst the locals, for sure. Hurrying to cut her mother off before she got started on in-depth questions, Emma said, 'Grace weighs three point seven kilos, has ten fingers and ten toes, and is cute as a button. Abbie's besotted.'

Nixon agreed. 'I saw her in the nursery on my way here. I think we could have a Force Six earthquake and she wouldn't notice.' His smile dipped. 'You're all right?'

The same loaded question her mother had asked. No doubt she'd hear it a few more times yet. 'Yep.'

He locked eyes with her, as if he was looking for more. But what could she say? Especially in front of her mother, who had had misgivings about the whole surrogacy thing from the day she'd told her family she was having Abbie's baby. 'I have no regrets. Okay?'

'I didn't think you would.' Nixon looked away, and got caught in the beam of her mother's stare. 'You've got one tough daughter, Kathy.'

'She had to learn to be.' It was so unlike her mother to say such a thing. Her family never talked about her past unless she brought up the horrible subject herself, which she rarely did. Why go back to hell when she'd finally found her way out?

Emma shivered. Her mum was certainly assessing Nixon thoroughly. Too thoroughly. Something she needed to stop doing. 'Nixon's my boss.' For some inexplicable reason that gave her a stabbing sensation in her chest.

Her mother nodded once, abruptly.

But Nixon surprised Emma with his suddenly widening eyes and flattening mouth. What had she done other than tell the truth? He *was* her boss. And one hell of a man, who had the broad shoulders to cry on and endless patience when she'd needed to let off steam. Those shoulders were filling her vision now, tightening her tummy in ways it shouldn't.

Then a deep yawn pulled her mouth wide. The day had caught up with her in spades. 'Sorry, everyone. I need to catnap for a bit.' She reached for Rosie. 'Another hug for Mummy?'

As Rosie obliged Emma glimpsed Nixon over her daughter's head. There was a strange longing filling those grey eyes as he watched them. Something she'd never seen before. Something that strummed on her heartstrings. Nixon was lonely for love? Was that it? Couldn't be. He could have any woman he set his eyes on.

But wait, wasn't there a rumour that he had a three-dates rule? He also shunned invitations from individual staff members to work social occasions, but that was probably sensible. Yet he'd asked her out. Strange.

She chose to be alone too, but that didn't mean she didn't want family and love. Nixon hadn't said a word about his family when she'd talked about hers the day she'd blubbed all over him. He'd only said he was too busy for commitment. What with running a small but busy emergency department here in the Queenstown Hospital, where extreme sports injuries were as common as the tourists that filled the town all year round. Being a mountain-biking addict alongside his busy job, he didn't have the time required for a full-on, permanent relationship.

Nixon might be surprised to know everyone knew he avoided relationships. It was fairly obvious when he only ever dated women who were visiting Queenstown, getting his testosterone fix without getting entangled. Emma hadn't been able to decide if she should've been flattered or insulted when he'd asked her out. Apparently she'd been the exception to his rule. He socialised without getting involved, so he'd have been a perfect date for her. She'd have had fun. It wasn't as if he were dull, weird, or afraid of his own shadow. Completely the opposite, in fact. Tall, built, fun, sincere.

Sexy.

Gasp.

Was it all right to think that of a friend?

Emma's heart slowed. Sadness rocked in and darkened her mood; she closed her eyes so she didn't have to see Nixon watching her with a hunger in his gaze that confused her. To her he was someone she worked with who'd become a good friend over the last few months. He was a man in need of a shake-up. Who amongst her old friends could she find to knock his knees out from under him? No one. What about—?

No one. Or—?

No one.

The thought of Nixon getting all cosy with someone she knew felt like a lead ball swinging at her head.

A phone sounded loud in the still room. 'I'd better get back. The heli's five minutes out,' Nixon said as he read his message. 'I grabbed a quiet moment to check on you.'

As her boss? Or as a friend. 'You want to give me a lift home later?' What was wrong with her? As if she wanted Nixon driving her home. But he'd ask less questions than her family.

Her mother got there before him. 'I can come back in whenever you're ready. You and Rosie should stay the night with us anyway.'

'Thanks, Mum, but I'd prefer going to the apartment, taking a long, hot shower and curling up in my own bed.' That was the truth, even if it meant having to stay awake until Rosie went to bed, which these days could be anywhere between seven and nine. The kid didn't get bedtime rules at all.

'Your brothers will be disappointed. Not to mention your father.'

Exactly. An inquest about her feelings was not on her agenda. 'I'll see them tomorrow.'

Nixon turned his formidable gaze from her to her mother and nodded. 'I'm going to be tied up for a long time with what the paramedics are bringing in.'

'What happened?' Emma asked.

'A mountain biker here for the Lake Hawea challenge went off the edge of the road somewhere on Cardrona while on a training ride and hit the rocks way below.' Nixon headed for the door, and paused, one hand on the frame. 'I'll drop by later to see if you want me to give you a ride somewhere.' A hint of challenge coloured his voice, which disappeared before he nodded to her mother, who was nudging Rosie towards the door. 'A pleasure meeting you.'

Then he was gone, leaving a void in the room Emma wanted filled. By whom? By what? She had no idea, she only knew her head and heart were all over the place at the moment, and that had nothing to do with Nixon and all to do with the baby she'd delivered not so long ago.

Yet she felt that challenge even if she didn't know what it was about. As if Nixon had handed her the baton and she needed to run with it. Now. When she'd just had a baby? When she did not need—or want—a man in her life? Forget her earlier longings. That had been baby-brain talk.

Baby. Her hands slid over her empty stomach. I had a baby today. And she's nowhere to be seen.

Abbie's baby. Not mine. Abbie's baby. Abbie's baby. My baby.

Emma cried herself into a restless, baby-filled sleep.

# CHAPTER TWO

Nixon Wright eased himself onto the chair beside Emma's bed, and, with his elbows on his knees, dropped his chin into the palms of his hands. The cyclist was in Theatre. He was done for the day. His own cycle at home beckoned but he'd told Emma he'd drop by before he left; hadn't told her he needed to check on her for his own peace of mind.

Watching Emma as she slept tugged him deep inside. Her short, light breaths lifted an errant curl from one cheek, let it fall on the outward sigh. Dark shadows resembling bruises darkened the pale skin beneath her eyes, her coppery hair striking against those cheeks. She looked small and defenceless under the covers, bringing all his protective mechanisms to the fore, making him want to crawl onto the bed and hold her close, keep the world at bay until she was ready to face it again.

He'd never seen her so lost. Oh, sure, she'd deny that faster than a blink, but she was confused, dealing with emotions she knew and expected and didn't want. She'd been brave today; so very, very brave. Not a hint of regret apparent, but there had to be a lot of tugging towards that baby going on inside.

Emma was a loving soul. Since he'd learned she was pregnant, he'd seen how she'd loved that baby growing inside her. Yet not once, even on those bleak days when she'd felt wobbly about it all—and there had been some, though she'd only ever talked to him about her feelings once—had she said anything to suggest she wouldn't give up Grace to her rightful mother.

From what he'd seen, Emma and Abbie had a strong, unbreakable bond so that had never been going to happen. Apparently the two women had seen each other through some terrible times. Abbie's husband had passed away from cancer, and from idle gossip in the department he knew Emma had been married to a violent man—which made him seethe with impotent fury just thinking about it. He shoved the anger aside. It had no place here, and if Emma had managed to walk away from that husband then *he* had no right resurrecting her history, if only in his head. She needed positive vibes.

Nixon's heart expanded. If ever there was an amazing gift, Emma had given it to her friend. Her generosity knew no bounds, but in the coming days she'd need someone to lean on and he was putting his hand up. As the friend he'd already been for her.

*Oh, really?* some strange, illogical emotion deep inside asked.

His phone pinged with an incoming text. Nixon read the message his uncle Henry had sent to all the family.

Hope everyone has a lovely time at the birthday party in Wellington this weekend. I'll be thinking of you. Sorry you can't make it either, Nixon.

Henry could be joining his children and grandchildren if he eased up on his belief he was doing his family more good leaving them a large inheritance than using some of his money to be with them for special occasions. Instead, he ignored the pleas to spend the money now when everyone could enjoy the benefits.

Guilt snuck in. It was brought on because his uncle had taken him in when he was six and raised him with his cousins until he left school. Henry had never been generous with money and especially not with his heart, but Nixon had been fed, clothed in hand-me-downs and given shelter. He'd always be grateful, but he'd have been happy to go hungry if instead there'd been open and happy love such as he'd known in his six short years with his parents and brother before they died in a plane crash.

*'Nixon, your mum and dad and Davey are not coming home ever again.'*

The terrifying words had cut him off from his family, from love and happiness. From ever giving his heart unconditionally again.

But had Henry giving him a roof over his head been his way of showing love? Fundamental perhaps, but that was his uncle's approach.

Well, he could do the same. Nixon texted back.

Book flights and hotel. I'll fix you up tonight.

Henry would go for the most expensive flights and hotel room, but, hey, those were the breaks. If it made his uncle happy then what did it matter? It was only money and he wasn't short of a few dollars. These people were his only family. They had cared about him as one of their own, looked out for him when he hadn't been able to grasp what not ever coming home again meant. If only Henry had shown his love with hugs and games and laughter as his own parents had, then he mightn't have felt quite so lost and alone.

Nixon's gaze drifted to Emma.

He'd cried off going away with his cousins and their kids, using a bike endurance he'd entered as his reason. While it was true, he'd also been reluctant to be out of town when Emma had her baby. He'd wanted to be around when it happened in case that despair and fear she'd once sobbed out onto his shoulder returned, stronger and harder to move past. He might've made sure she was all right when her waters broke and retrieved her bag from her car for her yet he'd waited 'til well after the birth to visit her, suddenly afraid of where his feelings about Emma were taking him. They'd become such great friends that he'd even felt grateful she'd turned him down for a date because when he walked away at the end of it, which he surely would have done, he'd have missed out on so much. While she was pregnant, he'd felt restrained about furthering their friendship. She'd had enough issues to deal with. But now where did they stand? He believed he didn't want involvement, couldn't risk his heart only to lose her when she decided she didn't need him, but…

But ask him why he'd felt he should be here and he couldn't find a satisfactory answer. Emma didn't need him at her side. They got along fine, and sometimes she opened up to him, though lately he'd pulled back, afraid of where this was headed.

*Be honest. You like that she talks to you about things she can't tell her best friend.*

Yeah, well, all very good, but all the more reason to pull away. That thinking could lead to deeper involvement, a place he wasn't planning on going. If he ever chanced falling in love with a special woman—Emma?—he'd want to be able to leap in, boots and all, heart and all, be open, have fun, share the highs and lows. He wouldn't want to be this uptight, afraid version.

His phone received a text. Henry.

Thanks, lad. Appreciate it.

No problem.

Had Henry shut down on his open loving side when his wife died in childbirth? Gone further into the deep when Nixon's mother died? Did he hold the same fears?

*Oh, man.*

Occasionally Nixon had wondered about this but had always shaken it off as wrong. He wasn't Henry's child, he'd inherited different genes, and his mother, Henry's sister, had been a happy, always laughing person. From what he knew and remembered. None of this had crossed Nixon's mind before. He could very possibly be a chip off the old block. Might've learned from his uncle how to hold everything in. They both kept their feelings close to their chests. Didn't rush around hugging friends and family.

*You hugged Emma earlier.*

Yeah, well, Emma.

Now what? Carry on with no hope of it being anything more? Or try to let go of the restraints and open up, risk his heart and see where that led? Instantly his belly tightened and his heart slowed as though it were withdrawing from this crazy idea, protecting itself. It was far wiser to stick with the current way of doing things. But was that truly what he wanted?

'You going to sit there staring at the floor all evening?' Emma muttered from the bed.

'It's a damned nice floor.' Grey vinyl wasn't really his thing.

She chuckled.

That chuckle crept into places that had remained cold since the day the social worker had picked him up from school and delivered him to Uncle Henry. The warmth Emma engendered made going for a diversion imperative. He wasn't ready to follow that warmth. 'Easier than deciding who to employ for the summer rush.'

'Which started a week ago, in case you hadn't noticed. The day the spring rush finished.' Emma shuffled up the bed, wincing. 'We've already had numerous broken bodies in ED from mountain day trippers going off track and getting caught by unseasonal storms.'

'I'll never understand why visitors to the region don't read the weather warnings.' Nixon stood to arrange the pillows more comfortably behind her back. Doctor mode to the fore. Really? Yes, really. 'Tell that to the CEO. We're up to our ears in patients and he's still saying wait. My problem is the doctor I want to take on won't hang around for ever. She's had another offer in Christchurch, a better one I suspect, but with a sister already working here she'd prefer our neck of the woods.'

'The joys of being the boss. Glad I'm only a nurse.'

'No such thing as just a nurse.' Especially Emma, a dedicated carer if ever he'd met one. 'How's the body feeling?'

'Like it fell off Ben Lomond, rolled down the mountain and finished up in a ravine. Just like your earlier patient.'

'That good? Want to go mountain-bike riding tomorrow?' he teased.

'Sit on one of those hard, narrow bike seats after what I've been through?' She shuddered and scrunched up her lovely face. 'Haven't you got work to do? Paperwork if nothing else.'

'I'm done for the day.' He gave an exaggerated sigh. 'The weather forecast predicts no wind and warm temperatures. Perfect for hitting the trail out to Jack's Point Pass.'

Emma shook her head at him. 'Your calf muscles must hate you sometimes.'

If he were open to more than casual friendships, he'd suggest they pack a picnic and take Rosie up the track out of Arrowtown one day soon. *If.* A friendship on that scale with Emma and her daughter could eventually expose his need for more and as he was her boss that couldn't happen. He never dated women he worked with. It got complicated when the three-date rule was enacted. He still didn't understand why he'd asked her out that time. Except that she was gorgeous. 'You decided where you're going to spend tonight?'

'I guess I'll go out to the Valley. It's the soft option but sometimes it's nice to let Mum take over with Rosie. I kind of want my family around too.'

Not him. Friends only. Not so close they shared everything. 'You don't want to stay in town without Rosie, do you?'

Emma stared at him, blinking twice and swallowing hard. 'No.' Another swallow. 'I need to hug and touch her, or just watch over her. I need to be a mum tonight.' Sadness flicked through her eyes and was gone.

It was hard not to reach for her hands, wrap his fingers around them and give her his warmth and strength. He all but sat on his hands in case Emma misinterpreted the gesture. 'You are allowed to be shaken up by it all, you know? No one's going to give you a hard time for feeling down about not having this time with Grace.'

Her left foot jiggled continuously as she nodded slowly. 'I get that. But knowing that and experiencing it are different. I'm not saying I'd change a thing. Of course I wouldn't. That baby's always been Abbie's. I don't even want another child. I've got the most adorable daughter and no time or energy to spare for bringing up a second child.' She stared out of the window.

She was an awesome mum, the kind he'd want for his children. If he was ever to have a family. He'd love his own kids, sometimes imagined holding his daughter, playing ball in the yard with his son, pouring into them all the love he knew he held inside. After he found the right woman and loved her to the edge and back—but that wasn't happening. He was a screw-up, had loved his family too hard and deep so that the loss had cut the ground out from under him, left him unable to understand who he was any more. Left him afraid to love without reservation. Hence flings were the way to go. Fun, carefree and over before the trouble started.

Nixon's heart pushed the barriers back in place that Emma didn't know she'd shunted sideways. What was he thinking here? *Get back on track.* Concentrate on Emma and what she wanted. 'Rosie's a lucky girl with a great mum. What more does she need?' Nixon felt that protective surge for Emma stir, the one that came to the fore at inopportune moments. It sat up and expanded into…? What? The need to look out for her shouldn't cause this sense of leaning too far out over a cliff, of hovering on the point of no return.

*Leave. Now. Go home and grab the bike, put in a couple of hours' hard pedalling. Break out a sweat, make the muscles ache, and silence the infuriating brain.*

His legs weren't behaving; they were suddenly lifeless, keeping him stuck on the chair. As though they were saying Emma needed his strength at the moment and he couldn't take it away, no matter the cost to him. Whatever the hell that cost might be. Just some strange, gut-tightening, emotion-expanding thing going on in his head, his body. His heart. *His heart? Get away.*

'She's unlucky not to have a dad.' She blinked at him. 'Forget I said that.'

Slap. Rosie's father. Nixon slowly leaned back in the uncomfortable chair. Did she still love the guy? 'How long were you married?'

'Nearly three years.' No emotion coloured her voice, or her gaze. None at all. Hiding her feelings?

Talk about derailing the conversation off post-birthing blues. Only problem was, he seemed to have hit as big a bump in the road. 'Sorry, I shouldn't have asked.'

'Why shouldn't you? It's no secret.' Was that anger firing up in her eyes? 'Broken marriages are as common as muck.'

'I suppose.'

'Alvin saved me the hassle of a divorce by getting himself killed in a pub brawl up north in Kaikohe.' Emma's mouth was tight.

'Jeez, Emma, you've had a rough time of it.'

'You have no idea.'

'Yet look what you've done for Abbie. You're tough, and kind, and full of love.' That love word was cropping up a lot today. Best find another subject to talk about. For both their sakes. 'Your mother coming back to get you or do you want me to drive you out to Gibbston Valley?'

She blinked, shuddered. Then finally dredged up a weak smile. 'Would you?' Relief began lightening those teal eyes, nudging aside the gloom that had overtaken her minutes ago. 'If Mum comes she'll bring Rosie and my girl has had more than enough excitement for all of us.'

An odd happiness filled him. Because she was accepting a ride with him? Pathetic. 'Are you allowed to go yet?'

'It's entirely up to me. The midwife has done her final checks for the day and says she'll see me tomorrow, so any time that suits you. I'll have a quick shower and change into something half decent.' She began easing off the bed, obviously feeling every movement.

Nixon stood up, rolled his shoulders. 'I'll go see how that cyclist's doing. He should be out of surgery by now. Back in ten?'

'Sure.' She was already digging into her daypack for clothes.

Nixon found his patient's orthopaedic surgeon writing up notes on the operation he'd just performed. 'How's our guy?'

'That shoulder is nasty, and he's in for a long haul getting back to—' Cameron flicked his fingers in the air '—normal. The skull fracture's of concern, though we're fairly certain there's no lasting brain injury. I'll operate again tomorrow to insert rods in his leg and arm. He won't be a happy chap when he comes round.'

'He's lucky to be alive. That was some fall.'

Cameron stretched in his chair and linked his hands behind his head. 'You cyclists certainly keep me busy. Shoulders are my expertise these days. You still as crazy on your bike as you were when you first arrived in town?'

Nixon grinned. 'What's crazy about racing down a mountain on two wheels? It's an adrenalin fix like no other.' He loved it, needed it at times. Used it to pretend all was right in his world.

'Could also be the end of you, is what else it is,' Cameron retorted. 'Your family ever worry about you?'

There was another question behind the obvious one. 'They're long used to me doing hair-raising sports.' His cousins had more than enough to focus on with their families and jobs without worrying about him.

'You ever think you should slow down?'

'Yeah, but then I get on the bike and that idea goes out the window.' If the worst happened then he wasn't hurting anyone else, because there was no one close enough to be affected if he didn't come home one day as his family hadn't. His cousins would miss him, as would Henry, but not in a life-stopping, future-changing way. He'd chosen to live like this. If he couldn't have love then he'd have adventure.

'You're mad.' Cameron was studying him far too closely. 'Find another fix, something less dangerous. Collect stamps or play bowls. Or…' and the guy drew a breath, warning Nixon he wasn't going to like this next pearl of wisdom '…a woman. As in a woman you go home to every night. They can be as addictive as anything else out there.'

'Bikes are cheaper to run,' he flipped back.

'You don't mean that.'

Did the guy ever give up? Nixon put some grit in his voice. 'You're right, I don't. What I meant is I'm not getting involved with anyone. End of.' He headed for the door. Time to collect Emma, whether she was ready or not. *And that's not getting involved?*

'Nixon,' Cameron called after him. 'Give me five and we'll go across the road for a beer. I promise to drop the subject of looking after your bones.'

'Sorry, already got some place I need to be.'

Disappointment warred with annoyance in Cameron's eyes. 'It's only a beer, not a lifetime commitment.'

Blast. He did not want to get offside with the man. 'I'm taking Emma out to her family in the Valley.' *Don't you say a bloody word.*

But he should've known better. This was Cameron. 'Watch out for her family. They don't like men hanging around their Emma.' Then he was busy filling in paperwork.

Dismissed. That was how Nixon felt. Cameron had got the last annoying word in. Except he was glad to learn there were people looking out for his friend. After the mistake her husband had turned out to be, it was only right her family would check out any bloke Emma became interested in. He could handle that. Besides, he was only her boss and a casual friend wanting to see her home.

Wasn't he?

If that was the case, why was he rushing up the stairs to the maternity ward with fingers crossed that Emma's mother hadn't come to pick her up? He'd be free to hit the road on his bike, put some wind through his hair if she had.

Yeah, but he wanted to be the one driving Emma out to Gibbston Valley tonight.

Glad Cameron wasn't around to hear that one. He'd be laughing for days.

* * *

Emma stepped into her parents' dining room and shook her head at her mother. The solid wood dining table was all but bending under the weight of food. 'I had a baby, I didn't run a marathon.'

'Everyone's here,' was her mother's explanation, meaning her brothers' girlfriends were hanging around too.

As long as she wasn't in for a grilling about her feelings for the baby, she was okay with their presence. They might keep the boys quiet. And she had wanted to wrap herself in family, right? What about Nixon? He'd chatted all the way out, saving her the need to fill in the gaps. Yet she'd known if she'd wanted to broach the events of her day he'd have given her one hundred per cent focus. She was glad she had accepted his offer of a lift, and what better way to thank him than dinner? Her mother would never, ever, not have enough food prepared to feed everyone twice over, so Emma turned to Nixon. 'Don't even try to get out of staying for dinner. Mum can be stubborn if she has to.'

'I do have to get back to town.' His gaze was cruising the banquet of cold cuts and salads of every variety imaginable.

'Might as well eat here as there.' Emma would swear he was drooling.

'But—' Nixon seemed to be having a battle with his stomach. He cut a look to her mother. 'Okay. Thank you for inviting me, Kathy.'

Technically she hadn't, but then she expected people to stay. Her favourite saying was 'Everyone gets hungry, I enjoy plugging the gaps.'

'You brought Emma out. It's the least I could do.' Her mum's smile was genuine. No hidden agenda, no lurking doubts, no worries about Nixon being with her daughter.

Oh, boy. This was getting tricky. She didn't need her mum getting all fired up about a man in her life. If, and that was a huge if, she stepped out into the dating world, she would not introduce the poor guy to her family until she was absolutely certain he could take the grilling that would come his way, but one glance at Nixon and she knew he'd handle it, might even expect it. Not that he'd be getting the opportunity. Dinner now and then he'd be racing back to town, away from her family and any risk of being slowly pulled in by the mantle known as the Hayes blanket—so called by one of the many strays her parents had taken in throughout her life. Not that Nixon was a stray. Just a little adrift. Alone.

Emma sighed. It was out of her hands. 'Sorry we're late, Mum, but I slept longer than I intended.'

*Remember, Mum, he's my boss; not a potential lover. Definitely not a future husband.*

One of those had already been one too many. She would never marry again, even if—heaven forbid—she did fall in love and move in with a guy. She was Emma Hayes for ever.

Her mother shrugged. 'No problem.'

Oh, boy, again. Emma spun away from her mother's knowing look and said, 'Nixon, you'd better meet everyone else.'

'Why does that sound like a threat?' he asked, sounding and looking as comfortable as any man could when about to walk into the bull's paddock. Could he be a skilled bull tamer? She was about to find out.

Out on the back deck she said, 'Hey, Dad, everyone, I'd like you to meet Nixon from work. He gave me a ride out here,' she added pointlessly, more in a pickle than Nixon appeared to be.

'Nixon,' Rosie shrieked from the swing. 'You came.'

'Hey, Rosie. Of course I did.'

The handshakes were testing, and the locked-eye looks

were designed to undermine any man not strong enough to withstand a tsunami of questions and probes.

Nixon took it all on the chin, smiling and individually acknowledging her father and brothers, Shaun and Daniel, then the girlfriends. 'Glad to know we're all on the same side when it comes to Emma.'

That had each of them tipping their heads back and staring at him before smiles broke out on their faces, as if they shared some man secret or something. Even Shaun's girlfriend was getting in on the act. Emma had the distinct feeling she'd missed the point and should head back inside to help her mother. At least she'd feel at home in the large, country-style kitchen with her mum, her lack of cooking skills excepted.

'Hey, Em, how're you feeling?' Daniel asked, not quite taking his probing gaze off Nixon. 'I presume you're sore.'

'Tired, and still all right with what I've done,' she said pointedly. Just in case there were any misconceptions going round that she might be howling on the inside for baby Grace. Right now it was the physical aspects of giving birth making her uncomfortable. A dull, throbbing ache in places best not sat on or pressed too hard a constant reminder that her day hadn't been about helping patients and all about giving Abbie a daughter. 'I'm going inside.'

*Don't kill Nixon, or hold him over a flame while I'm gone.*

'Nixon would probably enjoy a beer.' Her parents might own a vineyard but beer was the preferred pre-dinner beverage with the men.

'I like him,' her mum told her the moment she'd checked Nixon hadn't followed Emma back to the kitchen. 'He comes across as solid and kind and honest.'

That made him sound a tad boring, and Nixon was anything but. 'All of the above as well as a bit of a daredevil on his bike apparently. Also, he backs people when they're being wronged.' As he had her when one of the nurses had criticised her for carrying Abbie's baby. That day, she'd heard for the first and only time real anger in Nixon's voice, seen it in his tense body and taut shoulders. That was when their friendship had taken a step further along the sliding scale of acquaintances to soulmates. It also helped that he was deep, funny, and a little bit lonely. And, damn it, sexy. There, she'd admitted it again. And he still wasn't going to become anything more than who he already was. A friendly, caring boss. Saying it often enough would stop these errant thoughts popping up. Thinking of him as sexy was not a good move. But how to stop?

Little crinkles appeared at the corners of her mother's eyes. 'Just how friendly are you two?'

'Drop it, Mum. Please? I'm tired and sore and want to eat dinner before hitting the pillow.' Suddenly, curling up in her old bed, curtains shut tight, pillow tugged around her neck, and her eyes and ears closed so she became completely and utterly alone was all she wanted. To try and relax, to let go all pretence that today had been easy. To be able to study every moment again, to look at everything from all angles without anyone twittering in her ear saying how great she was for what she'd done. She wanted to hold the unabridged facts and emotions and absorb the truth of it all. Only then would she fully accept the birth was over, Grace was not hers, and she had her own life to be getting on with.

Her mother's arm was around her shoulder, tugging her close to that chest she'd always gone to in times of sadness growing up. 'Give yourself time, Em.'

'Can everyone see through me?' *Blink, blink.*

'We know you well.' Her mum's smile was lopsided. 'I'm thinking Nixon might too.'

Her shoulders sagged. Her mum was not one for letting go a bone once it was between her jaws. She conceded, 'He does seem more understanding than most men I've met.'

'Which makes him a treasure.'

Emma slipped free and slid her hands down her tee shirt over her heavy, full breasts and onto her flabby stomach. 'He doesn't belong in the local museum, nor does he have a place in my life. Nor I in his. We're too different. Seriously, Mum, I want you to drop this because nothing is going to come of it. I don't want it to. I'm not ready to get involved with a man again.' She only had to shut her eyes and she could see Alvin's rage as his fist slammed into her stomach. Until images like that one went away, she'd never be ready to give her heart again or to put her safety in another man's hands. Though if there was one thing she knew for certain it was that Nixon would not hurt her physically.

'I want you to be happy.' Her mum always got the last word. Or so she thought.

'Me too, Mum. Me too. And you know what? I am. I don't need a man to make me happy. I have to do that for myself otherwise I have nothing to offer.'

'Fair enough.'

Huh? The fact that was all her mum was saying rang alarm bells. The subject of Nixon was clearly not over, merely on the shelf for another day.

Over dinner, Nixon answered questions about himself without giving too much away—a fact the male members of her family seemed to grasp and accept. The guy was allowed his privacy as long as it didn't hurt Emma, was the silent message. It didn't matter that Emma reiterated bluntly that they had no right subjecting her friend to this. She was ignored. Her brothers and her father could be pains in the backside, and yet she understood they worried about her. These were the men who had run Alvin out of town with the promise of pain if he ever so much as thought about returning. *So, sorry, Nixon, but welcome to my family. Take them as you find them, or leave.*

Glancing across the table, she met his scrutiny and knew

he'd received her message loud and clear even when she'd been staring at her clasped hands in her lap. He nodded, smiled that smile that lately had begun taking on a tummy-tugging element, and remained in his seat. He was staying.

The only problem was that tummy-tugging smile caused an ache in her solar plexus. Post-birth pains? Not likely to be anything else. Not longing for something special with Nixon? Emma pushed her plate aside still over half full. 'My appetite's done a bunk.'

Shaun stopped eating to stare at her. 'You're kidding, right?'

She shook her head. 'Favourite food and all, I can't take another mouthful.' Something was cutting off her throat, refusing to allow food past, and what little had gone down before was bricks in her stomach.

'Nixon, you're a doctor. Take her temperature,' said her smart-ass brother, Daniel.

Nixon was still watching her; summing her up, she suspected. There was that astute, didn't-miss-a-thing glint in his gaze. 'You're all right?' he asked quietly, making her brother sound louder than ever.

'I feel like I've been run over by a bus, but medically I'm fine. Think I'll go to bed. Sorry to be disappearing on you, Nixon, when you've only just met this lot, but I doubt I can keep my eyes open much longer.'

'We'll look after him.' Shaun grinned.

That was what she was afraid of. 'Don't feel bad if you want to bolt while you can,' she told Nixon as she clambered to her feet.

'I've had a glimpse of what's for dessert and I'm staying.' His smile was soft and enveloped her in hope and a longing for what she'd sworn off. A good sleep and she'd be back on track, no left-field ideas knocking her sideways.

Through the haze filling her skull she heard her father say, 'In other words, he's no coward, this friend of yours.'

*Thanks, Dad.*

At the moment, she needed reminding of that as much as her mum did. Especially while this longing for something—someone—squeezed her tight and forced the air from her lungs. 'Goodnight everyone,' she muttered as she headed down the hall, aiming for the bathroom, ignoring the tears pouring down her face.

Crying wasn't a rarity for her. There'd been too many times when she'd not been able to stop in the past.

But not knowing why she was crying was new. And unsettling. All in all, it had been a huge day. Now she wanted it gone, finished, wrapped up and delivered, like the baby, and tomorrow's sun coming up, bringing the beginning of the rest of her life.

# CHAPTER THREE

'GRACE'S FACE IS red but she's pretty.' Rosie bounced up and down in her car seat as much as the safety belts allowed while they headed to school for a special trip to see the llamas.

'Isn't she?' Emma swallowed a yawn. There'd been little deep sleep last night, more a smattering of moments of not being aware and many long, agonising minutes of being fully alert and trying to ignore the emptiness in her heart. No, not in her heart because the baby would always be in her life one way or another. In her maternal soul, perhaps. She had carried the child and her body wasn't ready to let her forget it. But she would—in the nicest possible way. During the pregnancy, she'd talked to other women around the country who'd been a mummy tummy and everyone had said they'd been able to move past this feeling within a few weeks. It'd continue to give her nudges but those would come less often as time passed. It seemed that women who were able to interact with the baby had better outcomes more quickly.

Her phone played 'Jingle Bells', and Rosie clapped her hands. 'Santa's coming to town. He's bringing me presents.'

A glance at the screen. Nixon. Pulling over to the side of the road, she answered. 'Hi.' *Why are you calling me?*

*You don't usually get in touch outside work.* 'You got home all right after the inquisition?'

Maybe he was phoning to demand compensation.

A deep-bellied laugh rumbled into her ear, and sent waves of warmth—make that heat—to her toes and tummy. No, couldn't be. This was Nixon, Mr Super Avoidance. And she was Ms Super Avoidance. Concentrate. Nixon's talking.

'Checking how you are this morning.'

'Doing good.'

'I hope you're not rushing things. You're officially on leave now.'

'Thanks. Hopefully I'll be up to light duties and part-time hours not too far away. I'll get sick of my own company pretty damned soon I reckon.' Through sheer determination, her body would handle returning to the department more easily than her head and heart.

His boss voice switched off. 'Where are you now?'

Did it matter? Nixon didn't usually want to know what she did in her own time. It wasn't as though she was leading an exciting double life. No, she was a single mother of a loud and boisterous five-year-old, nothing more. Or less. But it was kind of nice he cared. 'I'm dropping Rosie at school to go on a short trip to see llamas.'

'On a Saturday?'

'It was meant to be last Wednesday but weather wrecked the plans. The kids were so disappointed the trip is happening today with some parents going along as help. I'm sure they're going to hear all about the new baby.'

'How do you feel about that?'

'Had to happen. It's not as though people didn't know I was pregnant with Abbie's baby. Though there is the sister factor to work out. Are these girls sisters or not? Abbie and I reckon they are.' They'd sort it but not today. Today she couldn't make Rosie's toast without burning it, twice.

'Rosie's a bit young to understand any of that,' Nixon surmised.

'Bang on.' He wasn't having any trouble with straight thinking, so she couldn't blame the hot weather for the mess in her head. 'Rosie met Grace and had a cuddle as soon as Daniel dropped us off this morning. There was no stopping the little minx from racing straight inside where Abbie was happy to oblige.' Emma released a tired giggle. 'You'll never believe who else was visiting, looking like he'd already received his Christmas present. Callum.' The speed at which Abbie's life had turned around was mindboggling. And wonderful. 'He's proposed, and Abbie's accepted.' Lucky girl. What a day she'd had yesterday. 'Everything's coming together for her at last.' Her sigh was not filled with envy. Okay, maybe a teeny bit.

'Fantastic news. They're meant for each other.'

'They are. Callum's besotted with Grace. Anyone would think she was his and he'd done all the hard yards.'

'We blokes are like that.' Then Nixon dropped a surprise. 'Are you going to be home around lunchtime? Thought I'd call by, check out my nurse and make sure she's getting back on her feet.'

'I was never off them.' Not true. There'd been hours lying and panting and pushing, but she knew what he meant. He'd said my *nurse*. Disappointment slowed her heart. Which was plain dumb. She was one of his staff. Just because he'd driven her home—probably because she worked with him—and stayed for a meal didn't mean she could expect something else. Then again, he was coming to visit her. Why this sudden yearning for more? For more with Nixon? Then it hit her. Avoidance. By trying not to think too much about Grace her head was filling up with thoughts about Nixon. That was all there was to these ideas and longings. Might be better to let Grace, and the sense of loss that snuck up on her when she wasn't looking, get in so she could deal with it and move on, no Nixon thoughts in sight.

'Hello?'

Where was she? Apart from parked outside the youth hostel. Nixon, and something about lunchtime and a visit. 'I'm here.'

'Say no if it's inconvenient.' He paused, then seemed to be drawing a big breath. What was coming? 'I've still got a shoulder available if you need one.'

Tears pricked her eyelids. How about right now? 'Th-thanks.'

'And a box of tissues,' he said in a low voice as if he really needed her to know he was still there for her now that the pregnancy was over.

'I've got to see the midwife at ten but should be home by midday. I'll fix us something to eat.' She would?

Relief underlined his next question. 'Your appetite's back?'

'With a vengeance. Think I had emotion overload last night.' And just like that, the tears spurted down her cheeks. A vision of Grace filled her head, held by a glowing Abbie, Callum watching on in awe. Picture perfect. Lots of love in the air when she and Rosie had dropped into Abbie's apartment. Really beautiful. Sniff. Her boobs hurt. Her heart was heavy. 'Got to go. See you later.'

'Emma, wait. Are you sure you're all right?' Nixon's concern spilled from the phone.

'Just having a moment. A good one.' Liar. 'Promise. Bye.' Bigger liar. She tapped 'off' before he could ask any more telling questions. 'Right, missy, let's get you to school.' She pulled out into the traffic, wiping the back of her hand across her cheeks. Rosie didn't need to see her mother's meltdown when she got out of the car.

'Mrs Watson showed us how to draw a cat yesterday. Can I have a cat, Mummy?'

Last week it'd been a puppy. 'No, darling, we're not having any pets.' So Nixon was leaving work during the day to drop by her place. He wasn't walking away from their friendship now that she no longer feared not being able to hand the baby over. Cool. She didn't want him gone out of her life. She loved hearing him laugh, the way he talked with his hands, how his eyes widened when he got all thoughtful, those long legs. Ouch. Friends, remember? Yeah, but seeing Abbie so happy she was fast moving on and wanting more in her life.

'But I want a cat. Why can't I?'

Reality moment. Talking about a pet was what was important right now. Why couldn't they have a cat? It would be good for Rosie and less work than a dog. 'We'll talk about it another day. Here's school.' She swung into a park outside the main gate.

'Mummy, there's Colleen,' Rosie shrieked. Her finger was jabbing the window in the direction of the gathering of excited kids.

Colleen and Rosie had become inseparable since starting school, and Emma hoped her daughter had found her Abbie.

Undoing Rosie's seat belt, Emma lifted her out of the car seat and handed over her bag. 'There you go, young lady. Does Mummy get a kiss first?'

'Yes, but hurry. I have to see Colleen.'

Blasted tears threatened again. Crouching down, she wrapped her arms around Rosie. 'Love you, darling. Have a good morning.'

'Mummy, hurry up. I want to tell Colleen about the baby.'

*Here we go.* People would be watching, talking about her—good and bad. She'd cope. As long as those who mattered to her were onside it didn't matter. Nixon's support and friendship being the benchmark. Friendship. That blasted word again. She needed to look it up in the dictionary and check that it didn't include hot zaps of need and heart-melting longing for a man.

Watching Rosie race up the path to her friend, Emma slashed away the tears on her cheeks. 'Sod off, mood. I'm happy with my lot.'

Had she been like this last time she'd had a baby? Absolutely. But there'd also been the Alvin factor thrown into the mix. He might've been gone for three months by then but she'd lived with a deep dread he'd turn up and demand to see his daughter, or snatch her away. It hadn't happened, but it wasn't until the police had arrived on her doorstep two years ago to tell her that her husband had died as the result of a fight that she'd fully relaxed the crippling fear.

'Jingle Bells' blared again. 'Nixon, did you forget you just rang me?' she choked.

'That's better. You're not crying.'

How wrong could he be? 'You rang because I sniffed a couple of times?'

'Just checking. See you later.' Gone.

Leaving her smiling and pinching herself. What was going on here? Would this feeling of excitement crash and burn as her hormones settled back in their cave? Had post-birth hormones temporarily heightened her awareness of Nixon as a man; a hot man? She stared around the car park, up at the sky, over at the main school building. There were no answers waiting to drop on her. She'd have to play the waiting game, to see the hormonal rush through to its end and look at what was left afterwards.

Nixon sauntered up Emma's path and raised his hand to knock but the door opened before he had a chance. Loud music spilled out. 'You're a rocker?'

'I'll turn it down.' Emma lurched forward as if she was

about to plant a kiss on his cheek, then as rapidly she pulled back, her face burning.

*His* face untouched.

'Emma?' He followed her through the apartment to the small but neat lounge where she killed the volume.

Her shoulders were tense, her neck stiff, and her hands now fists at her sides. 'Sorry about that.' She looked—fragile. Yes, definitely delicate. As if she didn't know if she was coming or going. Not surprising. The birth must've caught up in full force. 'I was trying to block out stuff.'

'Baby crying next door stuff?'

An abrupt nod. 'I'm probably adding to the problem as Grace won't be able to sleep. But I'm going up the walls and had to do something, and going for a run is not an option.' Emma's bottom lip quivered.

Nixon wanted to hug her, to send that crying packing, but sensed a hug might make things worse. He swung the paper bag he held in one hand. 'I got pastries from the French patisserie. That okay?'

Her lips softened, a small smile creeping in. 'I got some ciabatta from the bakery and ham from the superette. I thought we could sit on the deck.' She stared around the room as if it were foreign to her.

'Perfect.' Hopefully it would be further away from the baby's cries if they happened again. 'Emma, look at me.'

Her reluctance stabbed him in the chest. He shouldn't have come. She didn't want him here. But then she said, 'Take no notice of me. I'm all mixed up.' She drew a breath. 'I'm glad you came. I need sane and sensible at the moment.'

So he wasn't about to be kicked out. He wasn't sure he liked being labelled sane and sensible but if that was what she wanted then that was what she'd get. But as she headed into the kitchen his gaze scoped her body and that thick, wavy copper hair falling down her back, causing a pang of need to slide under his skin. Emma was beautiful. Alluring. What? Nixon tensed. What was that? Emma was captivating? Yes, she was, but he wasn't going anywhere with this. He recognised that she was attractive, but he wasn't admitting to wanting to follow through on that. Not likely. Oh, man, he was an expert in caution so what had gone wrong that his gut had tightened when he'd looked at his *friend*? Better get back on track with why he was here. 'About coming back to work. Don't rush it. We can cope.' She really was exhausted and would need time to recuperate.

'I know, but it's a bit confronting being this close to the baby so you'll probably see me sooner than later.' Emma sort of laughed. Strained and unhappy laughter.

It wasn't up to him. 'Why not move in with your parents for a few days? I know Kathy would love to spoil you.'

'And Rosie.' Emma sighed. 'It's like my family have always got my back and this time I want to be strong. I chose to have a baby for Abbie, and I need to see it through to the point I'm past these annoying hormones and accepting that I don't have another baby to raise.'

'I think I can understand that. But don't feel you're on your own. I'm here if you need a punching bag.'

Emma winced.

Wrong term given her history. 'You know what I meant. Come on. Let's eat.' He took her arm to lead her outside. 'You can fill me in on how you're really managing now that you've come back to earth. With a thud, I'd say, if those dark shadows under your eyes are any indicator.'

She swayed towards him. Where was this going? The scent of strawberries reached him. Her shampoo? Then she placed a hand on his arm and gave a gentle squeeze. 'What do you want to drink?'

'Water's good. Unless you've got a commercial coffee machine?' Strong black coffee was his weakness.

At last a full smile, aimed at him what was more, turning his toes and filling him with warmth. 'You see the size of my kitchen?'

He gave a perfunctory glance around. 'If you got rid of the toaster and kettle, put the tea, *instant* coffee and sugar containers away, we could make one fit. Just.'

'You're going to be visiting that often?' Those stunning eyes filled with happiness and laughter.

He shrugged up a smile for her. 'Who knows? Come on, let's go eat.' *Before I say something like, 'Hell, yes, I want to call in every day.'* He waved the pastries in front of her. 'You told me you're starving, remember?'

'I've munched on some biscuits since then. So not healthy.' She headed outdoors. 'Anything interesting happen at work this morning?'

'Surprisingly quiet really. Suspected stroke, sprained ankle and a couple of broken bones.'

'You'll never get away with that. This afternoon will be diabolical with every emergency imaginable.' Her smile was lopsided. 'Call me when that happens.'

'You're not serious?'

'Of course not. Even I get that I need to take things slowly, but it's so frustrating. Getting in the groceries is about as exciting as my day's going to get. Until Rosie gets home anyway. How come you're working today?'

'Braden got called out of town by his family.' Braden being his second in charge.

Plates and food were set on a tiny wrought-iron table under the pergola attached to her front wall. There was a bottle of water in a bowl of ice and mismatching glasses beside it. Emma winced as she lowered herself onto one of the two metal chairs. 'Right, help yourself.'

'After you.' Suddenly he felt awkward, and, worse, he didn't understand why. It was a bit like the very first time they'd shared a tea break in the department.

*You're kidding yourself, buster. This is more difficult.*

Back then Emma had been just one of the staff he was getting to know by having one-on-one sessions over coffee and cake. Now she'd become a friend as well as a great colleague, and a woman he couldn't seem to ignore, try as he might. A woman hurting and confused whom he longed to hug and kiss better.

*Like it's that simple. Let alone the consequences. Friendship ruined, working together awkward. Keep the kisses to yourself.*

'Thanks,' she muttered and picked at a piece of ciabatta without any butter or ham to make it edible.

Putting a thick sandwich together, he placed it on her plate and took the mangled ciabatta away. 'Eat. Properly.'

'Yes, boss,' she muttered.

'Give yourself a break, Emma. It's less than twenty-four hours since you gave birth, and it wasn't, isn't, the most usual of situations.'

'I'm fine, just making the most of having a few days off work, that's all.' Pick, pick, pick. Her finger moved faster, as if it was trying to destroy something. Him for raising the subject of Grace? It needed raising. How else was she going to move forward?

Nixon slapped some ham between two chunks of ciabatta and bit into it, chewed slowly. There wasn't a hope in hell Emma was about to start talking freely about what was eating her up. It was beyond her at the moment. She wouldn't know where to start. 'Remember the day I arrived in the department? When those two toddlers were brought in after apparently swallowing bathroom cleaner? Crying and screaming?'

Emma nodded slowly, and the eyes that met his said, *Where are you going with this?*

'Turned out they'd drunk gin from the mother's drinks cabinet, not cleaner, and they were tiddly.'

Emma began chewing slowly.

'The mother wasn't even embarrassed, more annoyed that the kids had disturbed her afternoon.' Nixon recalled the thin, young woman with more attitude than parenting skills. 'You picked up one toddler and handed him to me and said cuddle him as he needed that more than anything. Then you wrapped the second child in your arms and started telling a story, almost crooning to her. Within a couple of minutes both of them were quiet, hanging onto every word you uttered.' She'd had him thinking what a wonderful mother she'd make, not realising she already had a child.

That look was still fixed on him. 'So?'

He wasn't sure what he'd started out to say, only that the memory had suddenly filled his head and he knew he had to share it. 'Days later I met Rosie when she was dropped off. She was relaxed, funny, cute; well rounded. That came down to her having an amazing mother who knew what a child needed and how to give it. I understood then that those toddlers had had a special moment.'

'They don't get enough of them.'

'You've seen them since?'

'This is Queenstown. We all know each other, or of each other, through business, schools, you name it. The ones who've grown up here, anyway.'

'I've seen you give other patients you've known in ED hugs that have stopped the crying, or softened pain. Give yourself a big one, Emma. Or I can…' No, he couldn't. He might want to but he was not going to hug her. Hugs could be too involved, at least any he had with this woman would be, and involved wasn't in his vocabulary.

'I don't want to cry,' she snapped as tears burst from her eyes and streamed down her cheeks.

'Hey.' Now what? Nixon sat, transfixed.

Through the open window next door came the soft sound of a baby crying. Emma drew a long breath, her hands gripping her sandwich so that the ham slid out and onto the deck.

'You've only seen Grace once today?'

A nod. 'When we first got home from the Valley.' Her left leg was bobbing up and down, up and down.

'You're not ready to see them again?' Shut up, Nixon. Keep your sticky beak out of this. No, this was why he was here.

'Of course I want to,' Emma continued quietly. 'I want to drop in and out all the time like Abbie and I always do for each other. But this is different. What if she thinks I'm trying to hog Grace's attention, or that I can't let go, or…? I don't know.'

'When Rosie was born did you live next door to Abbie?'

'Yes, Abbie and Michael. Without them and Mum I'd still be trying to work out how to change nappies.'

'How often did Abbie come in here when you first brought Rosie home?'

'Seemed like every five minutes.'

'Did you mind?' Nixon asked.

'Of course not. I'd have been upset if she hadn't.'

'I rest my case.'

Hope spilled into Emma's worried gaze. 'You make it seem simple.' Then her shoulders lifted, her spine straightening. 'Thanks. You're right. I'm being a dope.'

'You're dealing with a lot. Go easy on yourself.' He stood and reached for one of the pastries. 'Now, I'd better get cracking.' The guy never seemed to stop working.

Emma turned to him. 'Nixon? I'm really glad you dropped by.'

'So am I, Em.'

*So am I.*

*Screech.* Tyres on hot tarmac. *Screech, screech. Thunk. Bang.* Glass tinkling.

The music stopped.

The air was too damned quiet. As if it were poised, waiting in anticipation. Something terrible had happened.

## CHAPTER FOUR

NIXON SPUN AROUND to peer down the lawn towards the street. 'Sounded like a vehicle hitting something solid.'

'Electricity's gone off so I'd say a power pole.' Emma snatched up her phone and charged down the steps and across the lawn.

Nixon was right behind her. 'Go carefully. There could be electric wires on the ground.'

The wires were still attached to the insulators, swaying in the light breeze, while the pole was at an odd angle, but nothing dangerous for them or bystanders. 'Call 111. Need power, fire and ambulance,' Nixon ordered.

'Already onto it,' came the calm voice of his very competent nurse.

Screams rent the air. Lifted the hairs on his arms. A young child's screams, filled more with panic than pain, Nixon thought. Hoped, anyway, and crossed his fingers to make doubly sure.

*Very medical, buster.*

Reaching the vehicle, he did a quick walk-round, making doubly certain a stray wire hadn't dropped to touch the metal with arcs of electricity.

'All good.'

Peering inside, the female driver appeared unconscious,

the steering wheel jamming her tight against the back of her seat while the airbag was all but smothering her.

'Everyone's on their way.' Emma was beside him. 'I'll see to the wee one.' She had the back door open and was feeling for the buckles of the belts that had kept the child safe. 'Shh, there. I'm going to get you out of the car, sweetheart. I know you've had a big fright, but you'll feel better out on the grass. Shh.'

The screams weren't abating, but Nixon had to ignore them while he dealt with the woman. If he didn't get that airbag deflated immediately she might suffocate.

'What can I do?' Abbie appeared behind him.

'Get me a sharp knife fast,' he called over his shoulder. It was an old model and wouldn't self-deflate.

Abbie was gone, not wasting time talking, her baby bouncing in her arms. She was not going to be able to help them much unless she could put Grace down.

'What's your name?' Emma was asking the child. 'Mine's Emma. You can call me Em, if that's easier.'

'Mummy, I want my mummy.'

'Need a knife here too,' Emma told him. 'This car seat's twisted and the buckle's not releasing.'

Nixon felt for a pulse at the exposed side of the woman's neck. 'The child got any obvious injuries?'

'Not that I can see. But he'll have been thrown hard against the belts. When the shock quietens he'll notice some pain. How's the driver?'

'Can't find a pulse. Yes, I can. Weak and irregular.' An event causing the accident? Or as a result of impact?

'I brought two knives.' Abbie was back already. 'Not sure which is best.'

Nixon took the pointiest and stabbed repeatedly at the airbag. Whoosh. Yes, good result. He held the woman's head so she didn't drop forward too hard. 'Emma, going to need you here.'

She was sawing at the seat belt. 'Two ticks. Need someone to try to calm our little man.'

Abbie stepped closer, her arms full of baby Grace. 'I'll talk to him while you help Nixon.'

'Can I do something to help?' a man asked.

Nixon glanced around, saw a gathering crowd and then the young guy standing near Abbie. 'Can you try to get that belt undone or cut apart?' He didn't wait for an answer, turning immediately back to the woman. 'Em, I don't want to move her until the ambulance is here and we can get a neck brace on but I need to see what the damage is.'

'I'll get in from the other side.' She was gone, and almost immediately inside the car, wincing as she hurried.

'Hold her head still for me.' Nixon tore open the woman's blouse and cursed silently. Left side of ribcage stoved in. Probable punctured lung.

'You need to check her pulse again,' Emma said. 'Her resp rate is non-existent.'

He placed two fingers on her carotid again. 'You're right. Got to get her out of here.'

'Mummy, I want you.'

Nixon flipped his head around, stared into the anguished eyes of the child—a boy if his fire-engine shirt was an indicator—saw the terror, and shock. *Felt* the fear. *Knew* those crippling emotions as if they'd happened to him yesterday. And the kid didn't understand he might be losing his mother. Didn't have a clue in Hades what that meant. How his life could be tossed up and down, round and round, with no chance of ever righting itself.

*Not on my watch.*

He knew the cruel blows coming to the boy if he didn't save this woman. Knew how love could switch to fear that swamped all emotion. 'Do what you can to hold her head steady and I'll get others to help lift her out.'

Sirens filled the air, the fire truck suddenly beside them

and men swamping the area. Would've preferred the ambulance, but he wasn't going to be picky. 'Hey, guys, here, now.'

'They'll have a neck brace,' Emma informed him.

She wasn't forgetting the important stuff. Not like him. Of course fire crews carried basic emergency equipment for patients.

Within moments their patient was out of the car and lying on the ground, and Nixon was doing compressions. *One, two, three, four. Come on, lady. Don't you dare not come back for your son. Ten, eleven, twelve. Do you even have a clue what it's like to grow up without your mother there for you? Thirty.*

Nixon lifted his hands, nodded to the fireman ready to squeeze air into the woman's lungs with a ventilation bag.

*Faster, man.*

Of course the guy was doing his job correctly; it only felt as if it were taking for ever.

One, two, three. More sirens. Six, seven, eight. *Lady, you'd better start breathing or I'm going to get angry. Your son is crying for you now. Think how he'll feel if someone has to tell him you're not coming home. Ever.* Twenty-one, twenty-two.

'She stopped breathing shortly after we arrived.' Emma was talking to paramedics as she stepped away to allow them access. 'There's a little boy too. He's just been freed.' She reached out for the child being held by the man who'd helped cut him out of his seat. 'Hey, sweetheart, let me carry you away from the naughty car.'

At least Emma was thinking straight. The boy did not need to see his mother in this state. Thirty. Nixon stopped compressions for two puffs of oxygen to be given.

'We have a pulse,' the fireman at the woman's head said.

Relief snapped through the air. Nixon glanced along

the path to where Emma stood holding the child, talking quietly, trying to soothe him.

*We did it, buddy. Your mum's alive.*

Though still in big trouble. Now to get on with saving her from those injuries. Hopefully not a flail chest. The compressions wouldn't have helped there but he'd had no choice.

As Nixon checked her ribcage he began to think luck was on this mother's side. And her son's. 'Let's get her loaded and down to the hospital. I don't think those ribs are as bad as first expected but I don't want any delay.'

'We've got her,' one of the paramedics commented as he attached leads to the defib, reminding Nixon that out here he took second place. These guys knew what they were doing.

'I'll see you in ED, Jeff. There's also a young boy who needs transporting to hospital.'

'A second ambulance is nearly here,' the paramedic informed him.

'You okay?' Emma was at his side.

'Sure.' Now that the situation was under control the adrenalin rush was quietening down.

Emma shrugged as if she didn't believe him. 'Guess this takes care of your appointment with the CEO.'

'Definitely. I'd better get cracking. Talk later.' Nixon shoved his hand in his pocket for his keys. 'You were great with that child.'

'Poor kid. I couldn't find any serious wounds, only two abrasions, but the head stuff—that's going to be hard to fix in a hurry.'

Oh, yeah. And if the worst happened then there would be no fixing him. He would carry today in his head and heart for the rest of his life. It would form the basis of everything he did from now on. 'Do you know if anyone's contacted his father? Or relatives?'

'The police are onto it.'

Being focused on saving the mother, he hadn't noticed their arrival. 'Good.' As long as there was a father to step up for his son, and the woman wasn't in Emma's position.

'You sure you're okay?' Emma asked, her gaze fixed on him, studying him intently.

Had she noticed his anguish? The urgency driving him to resuscitate the mother? Had Emma seen his fear? His need to save a boy from the pain and bewilderment he'd suffered? Please no. He didn't need other people to know how he still hurt, how he was still afraid he'd lose someone else he loved. He did not want Emma's sympathy. That would squash any sense of awe he might feel with her. 'Why wouldn't I be?'

'I don't know. You looked desperate while doing compressions.' Yep, she'd seen through his façade to the screw-up inside.

Where did that leave him? More screwed up, or letting go some of the fierce grip he kept on his emotions? In an effort to curb her interest in his background, he forced all emotion out of his voice as he told her, 'Of course I was. That woman's life was in the balance, and I had to save her.'

'Of course you did.' Disappointment tainted with hurt glared out of those soft green eyes. 'Thought there was something more going on, that's all.'

Once Emma knew his history she'd be in, under his skin, behind the barriers he held in place with sheer determination and not much else. When that happened, he'd be lost. For ever. 'Isn't that enough?'

Emma's gaze locked on him. 'Not for me. You're hiding something.' Her eyes widened. 'From me or from yourself.'

Nixon strode towards his vehicle, hoping she wouldn't follow. He'd love nothing more than to wind his arms around her, let her warmth push out the chill that had gripped him when the boy had screamed for his mummy. But he couldn't take the risk. What if he found himself wanting more and more from her? It would be like falling into something deep and dangerous from which there'd be no turning back; a place where he'd open up and expose his needs and fears and take everything she had to offer, and he wouldn't know how to give back half as much. He would always hold a part of him back in case he lost her.

*So, Emma Hayes, I am not going to be any more than a friend, a close one maybe, but not a lover or more. You deserve so much better.*

Emma watched Nixon charge down the footpath to his fancy four-wheel drive with its bike stand on the back. Those long, toned legs ate up the distance. He'd say he had to get back to the hospital in a hurry for that woman, and, while there was truth in that, there were other medics on duty. His unreasonable hurry was most likely to get away from her questions. She'd pushed him when he didn't want to talk. Something had been going on inside that clever head. Something deep and painful. Which was why she shouldn't be surprised he hadn't answered her query. Did he not understand how much she cared? How much she wanted to help him, as he had her? That was what friends were all about.

Wary, remember? Non-involved, remember?

He had no qualms when it came to asking about her past, her family, Rosie's father. None at all. Sure, he sheathed the questions in concern for her, but he still damned well put them out there. Almost as if he wanted to get closer but was afraid of where that might take him. He needn't have worried. She might be noticing him as a man, a sexy, desirable hunk even, but she wasn't going anywhere with this.

Back at her apartment she cleared the outside table. Nixon wasn't into sharing about himself, which meant no real closeness. Good friends shared some private details about themselves. Lovers a lot more. There were no secrets between two people in love. There was her answer. This had nothing to do with love because she couldn't tell him how weak and feeble the past had made her. She certainly wasn't going to explain how his care and concern piqued her interest, made her think there was a life out there involving a man—love, sex, commitment.

The baby cried on the other side of her lounge wall.

Her boobs squeezed tight, diverting her from Nixon and the improbable to Grace and reality.

The sound of Abbie murmuring sweet nothings to her daughter drifted through from her open windows to Emma's straining ears. Nothing like a baby's cry to hit her heart, pull on the strings.

Emma crossed her arms carefully over her breasts. *Down, girls, down. Not your job to feed Grace.* Sharp tugs of pain said it all.

She could go visit, maybe hold Grace. She had to if she wanted to move forward, past this hurdle of longing. Deal with this and put Nixon on hold. She was using him, if only in her head, to avoid the emptiness from handing the baby over.

She might as well deal with the real problem here. It was baby Grace who made her ache with pain and longing and love, not Nixon. With a huff she headed across the lawn and up the steps to Abbie's deck. Never before had she been reluctant to drop in on her friend, while at the same time she couldn't wait, needing to reassure herself they were still on the same page, that nothing had changed between them.

'Hey, how're you doing?' she asked softly as she stepped inside the apartment identical to hers in size and layout and the exact opposite in décor. While Emma went for soft and feminine Abbie had chosen a strong modern style.

Abbie looked up with wonder in her eyes. 'Amazing. I still can't quite believe I'm breastfeeding my daughter.'

Emma's boobs were still doing that tightening, painful thing, but she just breathed deeply and waited until they got tired of the game. 'It's great for bonding. I still remember those feelings when I first fed Rosie, and many times afterwards. It's so special.'

'You want to hold Grace when I'm done?' Abbie was watching her too closely. As if she could see the need inside. No surprise there.

Suddenly the turmoil that had kept her busy doing unnecessary things that morning dropped away. 'I'd love to. And for the record, I'm fine about it all.' It was the truth, just not the whole truth.

'I know. Just don't push yourself too hard and fast to get up and running again. You're going to be pummelled with emotions for a while, but I'm here, okay? We can talk any time, about anything.'

'Someone else with nothing to keep their mind occupied but me and my problems.' What was it with people today? Was this their way of looking out for her? To tell her what to do, and how and when?

'Nixon giving you grief, was he? I couldn't believe it when he turned up earlier. Then again, maybe I could.'

The downside of living next to each other was they both knew who their visitors were, what music they were listening to, and what was cooking on the stovetop. 'Just as well for that woman he was here.'

'You can say that again.' Abbie shuddered. 'That poor little boy was so scared. I hope he didn't see his mother lying on the ground.'

'Me too.' Emma watched Grace feeding. 'Sorry about the loud music. Hope I didn't wake the baby. I was trying to distract myself.'

'I guessed. Don't worry, it wasn't that loud. Maybe she's going to be a rocker because she wasn't fazed at all.'

'I'll move apartments before she's old enough to know how to download tunes.'

'Why did Nixon visit?' Persistent. 'It's not like he ever has before.'

See? Abbie didn't miss a thing. Two could play at that game. 'Callum left for work early this morning.'

Abbie blushed. 'He stayed the night—not that it was very restful with little miss making herself known every hour.'

'Bet she wasn't the only cause of lack of sleep,' Emma retorted around a grin. 'Did he get called in early?'

Abbie nodded. 'There was an accident on Lake Wanaka. Two boats were racing and crashed into each other.'

'Morons. No one ever thinks it'll happen to them.' In ED they'd seen and dealt with every scenario and nothing much surprised either of them. 'I didn't hear the helicopter.' Callum was a paramedic on the rescue helicopter.

'They came in while you were taking Rosie to meet up for her llama visit.' Abbie lifted Grace from her breast and laid her over her shoulder for a back rub. Just like an old hand. 'Nixon? Don't think you can avoid my question.'

*Hadn't thought I could.*

But she had given it her best shot, hoping Abbie had baby brain too. Got that wrong, hadn't she? Bloodhound Abbie never dropped a question she was bursting to know the answer to, and Nixon's visit was right up there. 'He was checking up on me. Brought some pastries for lunch so I didn't mind being looked in on.'

'Oh, right. His phone wasn't working, then. I hope you were nice and friendly.'

'Why wouldn't I be?' Emma could feel her hackles rising. *Down girl. This is Abbie, who says whatever she likes to you.*

'Because you need a man in your life, and who better than Nixon? He's got everything a hot-blooded woman needs. At least I presume he does.'

'I do not need a man. I do just fine alone. Okay, not alone. There's Dad, Daniel and Shaun to annoy the heck out of me with all their checking and telling me how to run my life.'

Abbie grinned. 'They're not the sort of men I was thinking of. A man, as in sex and kisses and holding hands and—'

'Shut up, Abbie, and give me Grace.' Emma reached for the baby and hugged her carefully against her achy breasts. This time the ache didn't bother her. Instead she felt right holding Grace and knowing she would be giving the cute little dot back to her mum shortly. Her hackles had returned to their normal position, quiet and submissive. 'She's gorgeous.'

'Absolutely,' Abbie sighed through her perpetual smile. 'Do you think Nixon's hot? Because if you don't I'll never mention him again in connection with you.'

She should've known Abbie hadn't finished. 'This is me you're telling that ridiculous lie to.'

The smile widened. 'So? Hot? Or not?'

The air limped out of her lungs. 'Hot.'

'Yes.' Abbie punched the air. 'I knew it.'

'Don't go there. Every female in Queenstown over the age of ten would agree with us. I am normal in that respect. Nothing's going to happen between single mum me and Mr Uninvolved. Nixon's devoted to his career and lives most of his life in ED. When he's not there he's outdoors on his bike. He's not the type to drop by for a glass of wine.' Except he'd sat on her deck an hour ago. 'He doesn't like knowing why people are upset or not coping with something.' Yet he was always there when she needed help.

The more she said, the more Emma realised she'd nailed

what was worrying her about him. She didn't really know Nixon. He appeared to do the avoidance thing yet made his shoulder available whenever she needed it. More importantly, today he'd known exactly why she was so moody. Too easily, what was more. Leading her to see through that reserve he kept in place more often than not. Had Nixon let her closer than anyone else? Still not close enough to talk about what put that anguish in his gaze while trying to save the woman. What had that been about? He'd been shaken up badly, off the Richter scale. All she'd wanted was to hold him until that pain and desperation disappeared.

*Get real, Emma. You're looking for trouble. Tomorrow, or next week, or next month, when your hormones are back in place, you'll recall this and have a bloody good laugh for being so naïve.*

Fingers crossed.

Abbie screwed up her nose. 'Wonder why he does keep himself aloof more than most people. Look at that three-date rule he's supposed to have. It's kind of strange when he can be social and always keeps tabs on his staff if there's something going on in their lives that's causing problems. No denying he holds a piece of himself back. An important piece, I reckon.'

Grace blew a bubble and Emma gently wiped the goo away. She was so cute. Time to change the subject. 'Thanks for understanding. I will move on, still hang around, and try not to watch you like a hawk over how you're doing with Grace.'

'You don't think I know that?' Abbie came and wrapped her arms around Emma and her daughter. 'Silly woman.'

'I've had some doubts over the past months,' Emma admitted.

'Knew that too.'

'Know-it-all.' Emma relaxed totally for the first time since Grace's arrival. There'd be days when she struggled with letting go but with Abbie being so understanding she'd make it through the murky patches. She would.

Nixon had made a valid point though. She shouldn't rush the process; she needed to deal with errant hormones and emotions as they arose, not tease them into existence and then get upset because she couldn't beat them into submission.

Abbie had more to say. Nothing new there. 'You're so generous of spirit to those of us you hold in your heart. You'd do anything for us. Carrying my baby was never going to be a stroll in the park but you did it, and did it graciously.' Abbie wiped the back of her hand over her eyes. 'If Alvin hadn't done all those hideous things to you and you hadn't had my shoulder to cry on, do you think you'd have given me Grace?'

'Of course I would've.' Emma paused, thought about it some more. 'I might not have known to make the offer, because I wouldn't have understood the pain of never having something I'd grown up always believing would be my right. But I would've said yes if you'd asked.'

'See? You gave me Michael's baby when I couldn't carry a baby to term. I love you to bits but the love you thought you'd have with Alvin, that raising kids and growing older together love, the thing you believed was your right, didn't happen. You understand loss.'

Where was Abbie going with this? She didn't have to wait long to find out.

'Nixon won't hurt you. I'd swear to that.'

'You're forgetting, I never pegged Alvin for the monster he turned out to be. Nor did you.'

'True.' Abbie's smile finally faded. She'd always felt bad about not working out what had been going on behind Emma's closed door during her marriage. Not that they'd lived next door to each other then. That had come after Emma had gone solo and started looking for her own place. It had been Abbie who'd suggested she move into the apartment next to hers and made her parents take Emma as a tenant. The move had turned her life around and got her back on track, this time as a solo mum.

'Hey, don't go there. I could've told you long before I did.' They'd also had this part of the conversation more than once. 'For the record, I think you're right. Nixon doesn't have a nasty bone in his body.'

'You've seen his bones?' A wicked gleam lit up Abbie's eyes.

'No.'

'I saw that. You want to.'

Emma screwed up her nose, and gave up trying to remain coy. 'Is it possible to have a fling—okay, sex—with a guy for as long as it takes to get the need out of your system and then walk away without being hurt?'

'For you and me, no.'

'Then this conversation's redundant. Nixon remains in the boss and casual friend category.' A sharp pain stabbed behind her ribs. Nothing to do with boobs that were full of milk not needed, and all to do with a longing she hadn't known existed until very recently, and which she couldn't—but had to find a way to—deny.

'Em.' Abbie nudged her. 'Don't be so hard on yourself. Or on any guy who comes along showing some interest in you. Your life isn't over.'

Said the woman who'd believed for a long time that her life was finished when Michael died. It was Emma's turn to slash tears away from her cheeks. Staring down at the gorgeous bundle tucked into her arm, she gave a wobbly smile. 'I have Rosie.' She didn't need anyone else. But there were days when she wouldn't mind a man in her life she could trust and rely on not to beat her up. And to love her for who she was. 'My life's pretty darned good these days.' She'd had lunch with a friend on her deck. That never happened.

She'd ignore the longing for strong arms and a warm male body tucked against hers lying in bed that sometimes woke her in the deep of the night and kept her awake for hours. It only happened occasionally. She could handle that. It was how she stayed safe.

# CHAPTER FIVE

ROSIE RAN AROUND the park, shrieking and laughing as only little girls did as she held onto the kite's string. 'Mummy, look what I can do.'

Emma tightened her hold on the wooden baton holding the rest of the string, staying in the centre of Rosie's circles. 'Awesome.' The kite dipped and came close to the ground before soaring on a chilly gust of wind. Summer had taken a leaf from winter's book and dumped a load of snow on the Remarkables over night.

'Do you think Santa can see me?' Rosie spun round and round, her head tipped back to watch the caterpillar-shaped kite until vertigo won out and she tumbled over, landing on her back, feet in the air.

'Hey, careful.'

'Must be all right. She's still laughing.'

Emma's head shot up too fast, and her neck cricked. 'Nixon?' Who else had a voice that lifted her skin and tightened her gut? So, the hormones were still out of whack.

'Heard you two were down here creating havoc. This one's just like her mother.'

'Naturally. All kids pick up some of their parents' ways, and as long as Rosie's got my better ones we're doing okay.'

'I guess.' Nixon strode across to giggling Rosie and

pulled her to her feet. 'You've got to look where you're going, missy.'

'Did you see me crash, Nixon? Watch me with the kite.' She was off, racing across the park, her little legs pumping fast. Once again her focus was on the kite as it began rising back into the air, and not on where she was going.

'I've got it,' Nixon tossed Emma's way and chased after Rosie.

'You need this,' Emma called. Just like her daughter, he wasn't watching anything but the kite, but he'd heard her and took the baton. Ignoring the flare of heat where his fingers brushed hers, she followed at a leisurely pace.

Why was he here helping Rosie launch the kite after a sudden nosedive into the bushes? 'How did you know where to find us?' she asked.

'Abbie.' Nixon stood hands on hips, his eyes tracking Rosie, wariness on his face.

'You weren't meant to say?'

He shrugged. 'It would've been better if I hadn't, apparently.'

'Abbie will want to live a little longer.' She wouldn't admit to being happy Nixon was here.

He smiled, and her stomach dived. 'I dropped by to see how you're getting on.'

'Nixon, are you coming to our picnic?' Rosie burst between them. 'We're going to have it after I finish flying my kite.'

He flicked Emma a silent query, and she nodded.

'We've got chocolate biscuits,' Rosie enticed.

'I can't say no to those, can I?' Nixon laughed. Very carefree today.

'Yippee.' Rosie was off running more circles.

Emma watched her as she said, 'About work, if it fits I might do some mornings later in the week. I can be the bandage nurse, fix cuts and bruises. Nothing heavy.' She looked up into his eyes. 'I'm going to start painting stripes on my walls soon. Purple and red ones.'

'Stripes?'

'Or a large snakes and ladders board.'

'You're bored at home?' Nixon hiccupped. 'That's why you're down here?'

'Sort of.' No. 'I needed to get away from Grace crying.'

The beginning laughter faded instantly. 'You're looking for diversion. Is this doing it for you?'

'Sometimes I feel a ball of tears building up and I'm afraid to let them out. Especially when Abbie could walk in any moment. She doesn't need to see me losing it. That would make her sad at a time when she should be happy.'

'You're feeling empty?'

Bang on. 'There's a big hole where normally the baby would be. It's not unexpected, but it's hard all the same. Then I see the love and joy in Abbie's eyes and the hole disappears for a while.'

'To come back when you're tired or Grace is crying.'

She nodded. 'I have to be patient.' It hadn't started getting any easier yet.

'You're being honest with yourself, and that's got to help.' Nixon stared across the park. 'You've got Rosie, too.'

'I'd be lost without her. I only hope I'm not putting any pressure on her as a substitute.'

*I'm being honest with you, too. Understand? I'm telling you how I feel. Think you could do the same next time I ask about your feelings?*

'Rosie looks as happy as ever.'

'Thanks,' she said neutrally, and waited for more comments on how she was doing, because they were coming. Plain as day in that intense gaze.

Nixon looked down at her, his steady, deep gaze making her feel warm and cared about. 'You're amazing, you know?' Then he blinked, as though he'd shocked himself.

Amazing, huh? She'd take it, even if it wasn't true. A girl could get used to compliments. Could even start believing them.

It still rankled that he hadn't opened up even an incy-wincy bit about his reaction at the crash, but she could've got that wrong too. Reading people wasn't always her forte. Sick, injured, frightened patients—yes. Joe Average on the street, in her apartment, at Rosie's school? Not often. She'd used to have that skill, but maybe she needed to start trusting herself again?

'Nixon, Mummy, the kite's in the tree.'

'I'll get this,' Nixon laughed.

'All yours.' She loved his laugh, deep and sexy, and, today, so relaxed.

Shouts and hilarity came from the other side of the trees where teenagers were kicking a football and some were throwing a plastic disc. On this side couples were strolling with toddlers and dogs. A typical Sunday afternoon. Enjoyable, fun, and a little bit dull, if she was being honest. But she was out of the house and doing *something*.

'Don't break it, Nixon,' ordered a certain little madam.

'Would I do that?' he answered around a smile aimed solely at her daughter.

*I'd like one of those, solely for me.*

Emma shrugged off the pathetic despondency. He was here, wasn't he? 'How did the endurance race go?' He'd mentioned he was doing today's Lake Hawea challenge during that aborted lunch.

'Cold, and exhilarating. Came in ninth.' Satisfaction flooded his face, those dark eyes turning charcoal. 'The weather knocked some of the contestants off their pace.'

'But not you.' He'd have been totally focused, snow, rain or sun.

He handed the kite back to Rosie. 'Try to stay on the

other side of the park. If it gets caught high up in one of these suckers we won't get it back.'

'Okay, Nixon.' Rosie headed for the far side, at the water's edge. Lake Wakatipu might look beautiful and inviting but it was glacier fed and dangerous for unsuspecting souls. Other children playing on the foreshore would be temptation in full dress for Rosie.

Emma immediately followed. 'Rosie, wait up. You're not to go near the water until I'm there.'

'Okay, Mummy.' Except she didn't stop.

'Rosie, stop.' Emma picked up her speed. 'Now.'

Nixon strode out, those long legs gobbling up the distance to reach her daughter where he matched her pace and redirected her as he chatted, as though he were used to wayward little girls. Which was fictitious, as far as she knew. He didn't have a clue. So he was a natural. All charm. Don't forget wary. A cautious charm. Yeah, she could see the potential in that. It won him everything, and lost him nothing. Nothing except involvement. Go, Nixon.

Nixon watched Emma helping Rosie bundle up the kite. Perpetual vigilance with her daughter meant she didn't do relaxed in her down time from the department. He was used to seeing her constantly on the go, watching, caring. She'd carried the same instincts into motherhood. Rosie was one lucky little girl.

Talking of luck. The young boy from the accident had collected too. 'The woman we pulled from that car wreck will make it with few consequences,' he told Emma.

'That's great news. And her son?'

'Paddy. His dad met the ambulance.' Paddy hadn't been on his own, nor had he lost his mother.

*He* had relaxed on that score. There'd been a sleepless night afterwards, reliving his own day of fear and reality, but those horrid memories had been overlaid with pride for helping another boy avoid collecting similar memories.

Emma walking beside him made him happy. As if they were right together. Whoa. Where was this going? Foreign territory for certain.

'Remember, don't put your hand in front of its mouth,' Emma told Rosie, who was talking to a Labrador.

'It's cute.' Rosie leaned forward, her hands clasped behind her back, almost rubbing noses with the dog as the owner told it to stay.

'Don't even ask,' Emma muttered. 'Not until you make up your mind between kitten and puppy anyway.'

A shadow, a brief glimpse of movement and Nixon spun around. Saw a disc hurtling through the air at head height. 'Watch out,' he yelled as he swung his arm to snatch the spinning disc before it hit Emma. Bloody maniacs using one of these when the park was busy with families enjoying the summery afternoon.

'I'm sorry.'

Emma's words barely registering, he flicked the plastic dome to the teen who'd thrown it, sending a stern glare with it. Then he heard her strangled gasp. 'Em? Are you all right?'

'I'm sorry. I didn't mean it.' Her words were halting and filled with—fear.

Nixon stared as Emma huddled in on herself, her arms wrapped around her body, her hands white where her fingers dug into her sides. What was going on? 'You haven't done anything wrong.'

'Don't hit me.'

Whoosh. All the air was driven out of his lungs by those three words. Without thought he reached for her, to hug her, to show she was safe with him.

She jerked backwards, tripping. With fast steps she righted herself, but still didn't look at him.

*Be calm, don't add to her misery.* 'Emma. It's me, Nixon. I am not going to hurt you.' That bastard had a lot to answer for. 'Emma, please look at me.' He stood still, his hands loose at his side—not easy when rare anger raged through him.

Her head lifted slowly. Fear from those green eyes sliced into him. Fear that began dissipating as she studied him from under lowered eyelashes. 'Nixon?' Her tongue lapped her bottom lip. 'Nixon.' Her relief was rapid and enormous, lifted her head further. 'Hell.' Glancing around the park, she took in where she was and who was nearby before her gaze came back to him. The fear had gone. 'Sorry.' This time it didn't sound like a plea.

'Now can I hug you?'

'Would you?'

She shook like a puppy in a thunderstorm. Every protective cell in his body held her from danger. His chin rested on the top of her head as she wept against his chest. OMG. Emma. This was what her ex had done to her. Hopefully her father and brothers had beaten the guy to a pulp. They were very protective of her. The other night they'd been friendly and accepting, but, deep down, how had they really felt about him being there with Emma?

'I reacted without thinking. I saw your hand flying through the air and responded instinctively as I learned to do a long time ago. It's something I've tried to control but there are times when I act first, think second.'

'Did that save you in the past?'

Her head moved back and forth. 'Not often. He was usually too quick for me. He'd be there hauling me out of a corner. There was never anywhere to hide. Best to get it over with than rile him some more.'

Nixon couldn't help the expletives that spewed across his lips. And got a nudge in the ribs from a sharp elbow.

'Young ears.'

Talk about being out of his depth. 'I was catching that flying toy before it hit you.'

'I never saw it.'

'That's why I put my hand up.'

Sniff, sniff. His shirt was rapidly becoming soaked. 'All I saw was a hand flinging through the air in my direction. I haven't reacted like that in a long time.'

'I hate that you ever had to.'

'Mummy, I want a hug too.'

Emma jerked in his arms. 'Rosie,' she sniffed. 'Of course, darling.'

Nixon reached down for the sweet little girl he was becoming too fond of and lifted her up between them. The three of them stood bound together by arms and concern and…

No. Not the L word.

That wasn't what this tight feeling in his chest meant. If it was he'd be pushing away. Loving anyone was dangerous. Loving these two in particular even more so. They could decimate him with their power to tug him in and wrap their magic around his heart. Give him the things he refused to expose himself to. He needed to stick to being fond of them both.

But he couldn't step away, couldn't lower his arms or deny himself this brief moment. Not of joy, considering what had precipitated it. But he felt good; that protective streak of his was wired and ready to hold the world at bay for this brave, strong woman. With a quick, barely touching kiss on the top of Emma's head he finally managed to pull away, leaving the child in her mother's tender hold.

'Why are you crying, Mummy?'

Emma rubbed her arm across her face and dredged up a parody of a smile. 'Not crying. I got dust in my eyes, sweetheart.' Placing Rosie on her feet, she looked across to the lake, around the trees, over at the gatherings of people. Everywhere but at him.

Hurt lanced him. Why this sudden avoidance? He'd seen her break down. They had this between them now. But he hadn't been where she'd been, didn't know what it was like to have the confidence beaten out of him. That could account for any number of reactions, and yet she was still here with him. He'd take that as a good sign. 'Do you want to go home now?'

'We haven't had the picnic.' Rosie bounced up and down between them. 'I'm hungry.'

'When aren't you?' A soft, sad smile appeared as Emma ran her hand over her daughter's head. 'We've got orange juice to go with those biscuits,' she told him, 'plus bananas and apples.' Tipping her head around, Emma finally eye-balled him. 'If chocolate biscuits and bananas are your thing then you're welcome to join us.' The smile dipped. 'I'll understand if you've changed your mind.'

'Hey, stop that. You're allowed a bad moment without expecting me to think the worst of you.' Now he understood her need to appease people over some of the least likely things. 'If you want to talk about it some more, then I'm here for you.'

'I've never been one for prattling on. It's hard, you know?'

'I imagine it is. But not with me, okay?' *Never with me.*

'You didn't like me mentioning your reaction to that little boy's predicament the other day, yet at the same time you think I should spill my guts about what's turned me into the blithering wreck I can sometimes be?' Astonishment glittered out at him.

*Way to go for the throat, Emma.*

'I'm a better listener than talker.'

*Glib, man.* Also true.

'Same here, especially with someone not prepared to

share what's made them who they are, not willing to open up. I thought we were friends, Nixon.'

He wanted to be angry, but he couldn't when every word she said hit the truth on the head. Instead, his heart was skittering all over the show. They were on the brink of something here, something huge. Something he didn't understand. Something he'd already stepped back from once. Now he tried again, took a pace back physically and mentally, saying, 'I'm unable to talk about certain things. I don't know how to vocalise my emotions.' Like Henry? Where had that come from? Was there any truth in it?

The astonishment softened. 'Unfortunately, the result's the same. You expect more from me than you intend sharing about yourself.' They'd reached her little car and she flicked the locks before facing him. 'I can't work like that, Nixon. For me it takes a lot to trust someone and I've found that with you, but I need the same back.'

Another truth slammed him. 'I do trust you, Emma.'

'You want to explain why you were so desperate to save the boy's mother? Apart from that you're a doctor and you want to save everyone.'

Forcing his mouth open to answer her, to give her what she was asking for, he found that nothing came out. Not a word. Zip. *Nada.* Bloody hell.

*Say something...anything.*

*No, not anything. Emma will turn her back on me. For ever.*

'I see.' Her body slumped. 'Come on, Rosie. We'll take our picnic back down to the lake's edge.' She lifted the lid of the boot, retrieved a shopping bag and slammed the boot shut. Pinged the locks. Held her hand out to Rosie. 'Let's go.'

'Nixon, race me to the water.' Rosie didn't pick up on the tension crackling in the air.

Emma didn't acknowledge him, kept walking away.

Her hand gripped her daughter's tight, the bag swinging hard in her other hand.

With every step she took, cracks opened deep inside him. He couldn't drag his eyes away from that tight, straight back, those short, sharp steps. He'd hurt Emma as hard as one of her ex's fists had. He took a step after her. Stopped. This needed thinking through, not some rash compromise he couldn't fulfil. Getting it wrong would only compound the hurt.

Pain flared in his chest, as if his heart had been sliced in two. But love had nothing to do with this breakdown in communication. He liked Emma a lot, admired her strength and bravery, enjoyed being with her, wanted to spend more time with her, but love didn't—couldn't—feature. He'd shut that emotion down for so long, so deep, it was beyond being resurrected.

Chocolate biscuits and bananas weren't going to be a sweet fix for what ailed him. He turned away, aiming for his vehicle. What was required for that was impossible.

He would go back to being her boss and hopefully, eventually, they'd put this behind them and return to their comfortable friendship. Some time in the not too distant future. Only problem with that scenario—his body craved intimacy with hers. Got hot and flustered at the sight of those lush curves, the swell of her breasts, that copper-shaded hair spilling down to her waist, the multitude of expressions flitting across her face. Oh, yes, he wanted Emma Hayes as he'd never wanted a woman before. Friends? Baloney. Not any more.

Emma glanced over her shoulder as Nixon all but ran to his four-wheel drive. He was so desperate to get away from her he hadn't said goodbye to Rosie. That stunk. Her daughter had done nothing wrong.

*Did I? By being honest did I wrong Nixon?*

For once, tears did not appear to track down her face. Sure, she wanted to cry, loud and ferociously, to shout at Nixon that he was wrong to keep everything so locked up.

But how could she when she was guilty of the same thing? Her family had often heard about her marriage and the horrors it held. Abbie more often. But they knew her, they'd been there all of her life so naturally she turned to them when she finally opened her gob.

She doubted Nixon had ever talked about what was eating at him. Not to a soul. There mightn't have been anyone to tell, so he'd become a master at keeping quiet. No denying that horror and determination in his eyes the other day when he'd looked at the little boy screaming for his mother. But talk about it? About as likely as winning the lotto.

Then it hit her. Hard. Did Nixon know how it felt to lose his mother at a young age?

Emma's stomach sucked in. That was it. Had to be. Or, if not his mother, then his dad or someone very close. Whoever it had been, the raw pain that had been there at that crash site spoke of loss. A loss he'd been determined to prevent Paddy learning. It had been in Nixon's actions, his steady, determined compressions and dark voice counting to thirty. Paddy had not been about to lose his mother if Nixon had anything to do with it.

He'd beaten the odds, brought the woman back from death's door. Apparently she'd coded in Resus too and again Nixon had been her saviour. Driven by those ghosts, Emma bet.

'You're holding too tight.' Rosie tugged at their joined hands.

'Sorry, sweetheart.' She looked around for an available picnic table and came up short. 'Let's sit on the grass and have some biccies.' An engine started up, probably Nixon leaving. So he wasn't coming back to join them. Not today. Probably never.

Rosie had other ideas and was waving frantically towards the car park. 'Doesn't Nixon like chocolate, Mummy?'

'I'll eat his.'

If only life were so easy. Emma wished hard for Rosie to know only this sun-kissed version for many more years. She hated that one day her sweet little girl would learn that not everything went her way, that sometimes things went belly up very badly.

'Can I call my puppy Nixon?'

Despite everything, Emma could not stop a shout of laughter.

*No, you can't.*

'You're not getting a puppy.'

*But if you do I'll make sure it's a bitch so you have to think of a girly name.*

'I will one day.'

Shades of her own determination as a young girl were shining through more often lately. Where had that determination gone when she'd needed it the most? Into the mine of pain riding on a hard fist. That was where. Now she was getting closer to a man determined to keep her on the edge of his life who at the same time kept dropping in as though he couldn't stay away. What was going on between them? She was seeing possibilities for a new, happier life, shared with someone she might one day care a lot about. But every time hope lifted, Nixon went and proved how wrong she was. He did not want to get involved.

'Right, let's eat.' Swallowing was going to be difficult when there was a lump of bewilderment and disappointment in her throat, but she'd give it her best shot. Chin up. Tomorrow she might drop into work and apologise to Nixon for raising an obviously painful subject. Then she'd put on her mother hat to go pick Rosie up from school, cook dinner and go to bed to get up in the morning and start all over. By the end of the week the routine would surely have settled her down on all fronts. Baby hormones needed to start backing off and give her breasts a break, and then her head space could calm down and return to being rational.

The same needed to happen with the yearnings for Nixon that cranked up whenever she was around him. They had to go away so she could get on with her comfortable, safe, single-mother life.

Except she'd acted totally out of character when she'd stood up to Nixon about his reactions to that boy's mother's situation. Where had the cowering, be-nice-or-get-hit woman gone? She'd actually told him what she thought, and then watched him walk away. Was she finally getting a backbone? Standing up for what she believed to be right and true? She sank further onto the ground, her bones resembling jelly.

She hadn't backed down when Nixon had got upset, because it was important for their future. Not that they had one.

Determination in spades. Yes. Good. Great, even.

So why did she feel so tearful and pleased and worried?

Blasted hormones. Hadn't taken a hike at all.

## CHAPTER SIX

'IT FEELS GOOD fitting into my old-size scrubs again.' Emma laughed at her reflection in the changing-room mirror, ignoring the stretched fabric across her breasts and the tightness around her waist. Slightly forced laughter, but hey, whatever it took to start out the day on the right note.

Her colleague Steph laughed too. 'Like you were huge when you were carrying Grace. You made most of the other girls jealous with your lithe figure right up until you gave birth.'

'For that I'll work twice as hard this morning.' And keep as far from Nixon as possible.

'You will take it slowly, and you won't go rushing around like a mad thing.' Steph got all serious. 'You sure you're ready to come back? I'm not only talking the physical effort.'

'Best you don't give me babies for a few days. There's no guarantee I won't have a crying fit with these hormones swirling around my system. Every time I think they're on their way out they give me a right old beating up.'

'I'm putting you on triage. You can't get into too much mischief there. No heavy lifting or pushing wheelchairs either.'

'Yes, ma'am.' Emma saluted. It was good to be away from those blasted walls in her apartment she'd been all but climbing with frustration. She was probably pushing herself too hard. It was Wednesday, five days since the birth, but she had to get out of the house.

She scanned the department for a certain person, while her ears did an imitation of radar shields trying to hear his low, gravelly voice.

'Hi, Emma. Surely you're not back to fighting fit yet?' one of the younger nurses asked.

'No plans on doing anything crazy strenuous but otherwise feeling A-okay, thanks.' Not spilling the beans about the head stuff.

'Hard to believe you've had a baby,' another nurse said. 'Look at you, all slim and attractive again. Make that still.'

Okay, getting embarrassing now. 'Cheers. Thanks for the vote of confidence. Can we get on with something, like work?' Emma looked over at the white board where patients were written up when they were brought through. 'Not a lot going on yet.' Getting busy fast had been the plan.

'Listen up, everyone.' Nixon strode out of his office, his mouth tight, eyes serious. 'There's been an accident north of Wanaka involving a campervan and car. The first patients will be here in less than thirty.'

'How many are we expecting?' Emma asked.

'Two from the car in critical condition. One's on the way in the helicopter, the other by ambulance. The reports coming in on the remaining casualties suggest arm fractures for two plus a suspected skull fracture.' Nixon seemed to be talking directly to her.

Seemed to be, because his gaze had reached her and stopped. But she was probably wrong. He had no reason to seek her out. She was glad that the confusion between them had gone, replaced with calm and, yes, damn it, that irritating caution. Caution she now believed hid past hurts. Emma focused on the scant details he was providing and ignored the fluttering in her belly. They had to work together.

But did he have to look so delectable with that stubble on his chin? Those broad shoulders filled out his scrubs in a way she'd not noticed before. Emma shivered as need clogged her veins. She'd been fooling herself to think this desire for sex with Nixon was going to disappear in a haze of reality. She wanted him. All of him. That was her new reality.

'Emma.' Her new reality spoke directly to her. 'Welcome back. Sure you're up to this?'

'Better than going bonkers at home.' She glanced around the department. Her world might be topsy-turvy right now, but here at work she knew who she was, and what was expected of her. And damn it all, she was more than happy to see Nixon despite the misunderstanding that kept arising between them.

'Don't overdo it, all right?' Nixon stood close, his steady gaze locked on her.

Closing her eyes, she drew in a long, slow, man-scent-laden breath. How had she not been aware of this before? Nixon had become more attractive and sexy and exciting in the time since she'd gone into labour. The tension gripping her eased off, replaced with a different kind of tightness. Sexy and inappropriate in the middle of an emergency department.

Looking around, she found something innocuous to say to quieten her body. 'I think Abbie's bringing Grace in today for you all to meet her. As long as she's not grizzly, which she hardly ever is.'

'I can't wait.' Steph smiled as she picked up a folder. 'We had a collection and put a basket of baby things together for them.'

The buzzer announced the arrival of their first critical patient, giving Emma an excuse to look away from those watchful faces so she could exhale and quickly swipe at a couple of tears.

'Emma, you're with me and Nixon until you're needed in triage. You can roll bandages.' Steph winked before handing out jobs to everyone.

Brushing her hands down the front of her top, Emma said, 'Right, let's get this show on the road.'

Nixon stood in front of her, his eyes tracking her hands on their trip down her belly to her thighs. 'About Sunday…'

'I'm sorry. I was out of line.' She waited for him to raise his head so she could eyeball him. But when he did she got sidetracked by the heat blazing out at her, and she forgot what she'd been going to say. 'We work together, we don't need to know the nitty-gritty about each other.'

His eyes widened with relief. 'You understand. That's good. I'd hate anything to come between us that interfered with work.'

Not what she'd meant at all. Her stomach clenched painfully around a lump of disappointment. 'It won't. I love my job and won't put it in jeopardy over something you don't want to talk about.' So much for backing off. She was protecting herself, her feelings, her heart. 'Here's our first patient.'

Soon she was in triage, time flying by in capsules of broken bones, fevers, chest pains, a probable concussion. Emma took readings and obs, made notes, reassured patients and sent them straight to ED or back to the waiting room according to the seriousness of their situation.

Emma wanted work to be a distraction from everything going on in her head, and she got it. When knockoff time after only four hours rocked around she was shattered. 'Hate to admit it,' she told Nixon.

His eyebrows rose in a quaint fashion. 'There's a surprise. Time you headed home to those walls you so want to destroy. Oh, what have we here?' He inclined his head at Santa Claus being wheeled in.

Emma chuckled. 'Been climbing too many chimneys, Mr Rodgers?' So much for going home. She wanted to help this man she'd known all her life if she could.

'Get away with you, girl. My wooden horse fell over as I was handing out the presents at the primary school.'

'So you were Santa at Rosie's school today. Rosie was that excited this morning I couldn't get her to eat any breakfast.' Emma found scissors to cut the red pants away from what appeared to be a very swollen ankle. 'Who's taken your place on the sleigh?' Disappointed kids were not an option.

'One of the teachers made up some story about Santa's helpers being busy so he'd do the job. The kids accepted that, probably thinking they'd miss out on their presents if they didn't.' No remorse showed in Mr Claus's face, just amusement at what a silly old coot he'd been, and flicks of pain whenever he moved his ankle, which he did too often.

'Are you always this restless?' Emma asked.

'Me? Restless? Like I've ants in me pants, that's me. Been like this for a while now. Night time's the worst. Wife keeps threatening to move me to the spare bedroom.'

Nixon raised his head. 'I'll check a few things while we've got you here. Any numbness anywhere? Walking tall or stooped?'

'No numbness, can't always straighten fully first thing in the morning. Getting old, that's all.' Behind the smiley face worry flickered, disappeared fast.

Was Nixon thinking Parkinson's? Emma shuddered, mentally crossing her fingers for this lovely old man, and plumped the pillows ready for him once they got him onto the bed. 'There you go, Mr Rodgers. Let's get you up here so Dr Wright can examine you thoroughly.'

'This is where I take over.' Nixon placed a hand under

his patient's arm. 'I'm not having Emma flinging you over her shoulder this morning. Can you call us an orderly, Emma? Santa needs to go to Radiology. I'll give him the once-over while you're doing that. And then it's time you clocked off.'

'On it. You take it easy, Mr Rodgers.' The brazenness was dipping rapidly, the man looking more and more like a wizened old guy. 'Speaking of your wife, want me to call her and let her know how you're filling your afternoon?'

'No can do. She's in Auckland visiting the grandkids and doing the Christmas shopping. Bet I'll need a second job to cover that.' His smile was wistful.

'I can talk to her for you,' Nixon added his piece. 'Or you can if you're feeling up to it.'

'No, leave it for now. Get me sorted first.'

Emma glanced at Nixon, saw her concern reflected in his thoughtful gaze. Something wasn't sitting right, but if their patient didn't want his wife to know he was here then there was nothing they could do about it.

'Orderly,' he murmured, a slight lift to those full lips. 'Then home.'

Flip, flop. Her stomach did its new dance routine as she hurried away. How could one man's lips do this to her stomach? Lips she hadn't kissed, or touched, or any damned thing. *Lie down, hormones. You're on the way out, remember?*

Nixon pumped his legs hard, the cycle eating up the forty-five kilometres out to Glenorchy. Sweat streamed off him, moulding his spandex shirt to his skin. Salt stung his eyes and plastered his hair to his scalp under the helmet. To his left, wavelets on Lake Wakatipu glittered in the late afternoon sun. High above, two paragliders winged their way over the water.

Idyllic. That summed up Queenstown and its surroundings. Idyllic. The best move he'd ever made.

A car sped past him, the wing mirror a whisker off his elbow. He raised his fist and vented uncharacteristically loudly and rudely. The driver couldn't hear and he doubted there were people hiding in the bushes alongside the road to note his profanities.

But damn, did cussing make him feel better. Lifted some of the weight bearing down on him from the moment Emma walked into the department that morning. He hadn't slept a wink last night for thinking about that aborted conversation she'd tried to get started. Why would he consider telling her what made him tick when they wouldn't be going anywhere with it? He'd got by for thirty-one years without discussing the day his family died, so what would be gained by opening that can of worms now? A sinking feeling was going on in his gut. Like if he didn't open up his life would remain in this holding pattern. If ever there was a person he might be able to talk to, it was Emma. She'd understand what had driven him to withdraw from loving people. Wouldn't she? She'd been to hell and back and was still a very loving woman.

Pump, pump. He was pushing as hard as he'd ever done, needing his muscles to ache and his head to shut up. And Emma damned Hayes still managed to sneak in and wave at him. As if she were saying, 'Don't ignore me, I'm not going away.'

*Yeah, got that in spades. We work together, and we both need our jobs, love our work, won't be moving out of the department any time soon.* He had to find a way to stop thinking about her all the damned time.

Push harder. The body wasn't complaining enough yet.

The first outlying houses in Glenorchy came into view as Nixon sped around a long, sweeping corner. He glanced at his watch, pride lifting his mood. Not bad.

Then his phone chirped and dropped his mood back to ground zero.

*Ignore it.*

Except he was head of the emergency department. That wasn't an option. He braked hard, the cycle sliding in the loose gravel on the edge of the road as he skidded to a stop.

'Hello?' If he sounded grumpy whoever was annoying him might go away.

'Cameron here. Your Mr Rodgers's ankle is all put back together with some shiny steel. Yanky's paying him a visit tomorrow once he's fully recovered from the surgery.'

Yanky being the resident neurologist. 'You agree with me?'

'That our man might have Parkinson's? Yep, afraid I do,' Cameron confirmed.

'That'd knock him off his sleigh if he hadn't already come a cropper.'

'Quite a character, isn't he?'

Nixon asked, 'So what's up?' Cameron wouldn't have phoned to talk about their patient unless it was urgent.

'I'm knocking off. Feel up to a beer?'

Nixon's mouth watered instantly. He couldn't think of anything better with all the fluid pouring off his body at the moment. 'Could certainly use one. Only problem is, I'm out at Glenorchy—on the bike.'

He hesitated. He didn't often drop in for a beer with the guys, but cycling wasn't banishing Emma from his head. 'Where will you be?'

'The Thirsty Pig.'

'Put one up for me in forty-five. Pick an outside table. I won't be smelling sweet.' Nixon stuffed the phone back in its pouch and took off for his destination, eager to get back to town and that cold beer. Just what a bloke needed after a bit of exercise in this heat. And meeting up with the guys gave him a strange sense of belonging as he spun around the end of the road and aimed for Queenstown. Not strange, more like comfortable. A welcome distraction from Emma. Damned good, in fact. It had taken nearly a year, but finally he was getting to know his colleagues outside work, pushing aside the usual hesitation he had about getting too pally with people. Queenstown was working its magic, drawing him in and showing there was more to life than being a great specialist and an aloof relative or friend. Was it Queenstown's magic or Emma's?

The front wheel wobbled dangerously and he fought to straighten it up without taking a dive onto the road. Pedalling hard didn't stop other questions popping up. Had he learned to be reticent from Henry? That'd been nagging him for days.

*Focus, man. There's a beer at the end of this. Think of nothing else.*

'Get that down your throat.' Cameron handed him a condensation-coated bottle moments after he leaned his bike against the outside wall and whipped off his helmet to join the surgeon and Yanky at an outdoor table.

'That's pure nectar,' he said appreciatively after pouring a third of the liquid down his throat. 'It's hot out there.'

'Only if you ride like a madman. Why do you do it?' Cameron asked. 'There're lots of ways of keeping fit and having fun without going hell for leather on two skinny tyres that don't look strong enough to hold your weight.'

'He's taken up kite flying,' Yanky got in before Nixon could come up with an acerbic reply.

The beer he'd been about to swallow snagged in the back of his throat. 'I what?'

'He what?' Cameron also spluttered, but then *he* began laughing. 'Kites? As in those things that are tied to string and lift off the ground only to crash back again, often getting broken in the process? I know I suggested tiddlywinks, but kites? For real?'

Yanky had plenty more to offer. 'There was a little girl attached to the other end of the string.'

*Think I can hear a phone call coming in. At the very least a text saying I'm urgently needed back at work, or any damned place but sitting here with these two comedians.*

'Knew there was a reason I didn't do drinks with the guys.'

'Can't handle the pressure?' Cameron gave him a shrewd nod. 'Would that have been a little girl with dark curls and a stunning mother?'

'Shut up, man.'

Through a roar of laughter, Cameron said, 'I like it when people take my advice.' He drained his beer. 'Your round.'

'Your advice, your orders.' Nixon stood up, debating whether to escape or buy some beers. The beer won out. He was parched. Also, if he left here then he'd just go home and for once his swanky house wasn't at all appealing. It was empty, cold—lonely. Digging his wallet out, he headed inside to the bar.

The guys weren't done with him. The moment his backside hit the seat he got a grilling.

'Emma Hayes, eh?' was Cameron's opening shot. The man sounded smug.

'Been seeing her long?' Yanky wasn't any better.

'I am not seeing her.' Then what the hell had he been doing following her down to the park after Abbie had told him where to find her? Taking her pulse to see if she was ready to return to work? If any pulse had needed reading then it would've been his. It had been out of kilter for days, starting when he took Emma home to the family farm out in Gibbston Valley. Or had it begun its crazy erratic beat earlier when he'd sat beside her hospital bed while she'd slept? Or back on the day she'd sobbed out her fears on his shoulder? The day he'd tried to pull away, and hadn't quite managed.

'Why ever not? Emma's a great lady. A good match for you.'

The beer soured in his mouth. Coming here was a bad idea. 'I'm not a good match for her.' He made to push up onto his feet.

Cameron held up his hand. 'Sorry, mate, just ribbing you. But for the record, I think you are. She's got history that needs patience and caring and understanding.'

'She does and all—from someone more settled than me.'

'I hear her family didn't run you off the property last week.' That smirk didn't suit Cameron. 'That's got to be a thumbs-up, if ever there was one.'

Seemed nothing was private around this town. So he'd redirect the discussion, find out what he could. 'You ever meet the ex?' One thing he'd learned about this town was everyone knew everyone if they'd grown up here.

'Stitched him back together once after a brawl he got into and lost.'

'Hope you went easy on the pain relief.'

'No comment. It was no surprise he died fighting. He was getting more and more out of control by the time Emma's family ran him out of town. She did well getting away when she did.'

Nixon's heart died. Emma had been abused. He'd known that, but was Cameron intimating more had gone on? 'Just as well the man is dead.'

'I'll drink to that.' Yanky nodded. 'Guess it's my round.'

He mightn't like how the conversation had started, nor where it had gone, but Nixon was glad he'd joined these two. He was unused to letting his guard down, but they'd taken the choice out of his hands and he wasn't offended or angry. It felt good to talk about Emma and learn she had so much support. Not that she'd ever ask for help from just anybody, but that it was there was good. The upside of smaller towns, he supposed.

He was released from feeling he had to protect her when there were already so many people on her side. Men like these two, her family, they'd been there at the worst. He was new on the patch. But damned if he could deny this gnawing need to guard her back—and that was even with the ex being deceased.

Just another person to do his best for. Like his patients. And colleagues.

Believe that and he'd believe a newborn baby could climb Ben Lomond.

# CHAPTER SEVEN

EMMA DRAGGED HERSELF out to the car, pinged the locks and opened a window to let the heat abate a bit before she drove home. Thank goodness for Fridays. This particular one had taken forever to get here, three four hour shifts, but at last she'd knocked off work with the weekend ahead to do very little.

Everything had caught up with her, big time. Knowing she'd have to work through her feelings was one thing. She'd expected them to be all about having a baby for Abbie, and the emptiness she'd feel.

But she was being held back by other, alien feelings. Wants. Needs. Hopes. Call them what she liked, they involved her future and how different it could be. Bringing up Rosie on her own, without someone special to share the everyday dross and fun, was plain hard work at times. More and more she wanted to reach out and grab the fulfilment of those wants, needs and hopes. Those were the aspirations she'd grown up with and they were revisiting, teasing, tormenting her. She'd sworn she did not want to settle down with a man again, then along came Grace and she was losing touch with that idea. Knew she'd been wrong. Slowly, slowly, pinch by pinch, the idea of love and more children with someone special was making itself felt. Uncomfortable. Disconcerting. Worrying.

No wonder she wasn't sleeping at night. Nor during the day, which had to be a plus for her patients at least. She slid onto the driver's seat and tipped her head back on the headrest.

'Emma, wait. You okay?'

Emma jerked upright at the sound of Nixon's question. He looked harried, breathing fast, concern locking onto her. 'I'm fine.'

He shook his head. 'This is me you're trying to fool. It's not working.'

No surprise there. Dredging up a smile, she acknowledged, 'I came back too early, but what else was I supposed to do? Staying at home all day every day would've done my head in. Thank goodness for weekends.'

'Which is why I'm here, though maybe I should leave you to get some rest over the coming days.'

He had plans that involved her? She sat up straighter. 'Doing something interesting can be as beneficial as resting. In fact, resting doesn't work—too much climbs into my skull to annoy the hell out of me. I need a diversion.'

'So what are you doing tomorrow morning? You and Rosie.'

'Rosie's at a sleepover at her friend's tonight and staying all day for a birthday party. Me? Washing, vacuuming, getting in the groceries. Exciting stuff.' She added a smile to show he wasn't meant to feel sorry for her. This was how her weekends unfolded; nothing new there.

'Do you like flying?'

What was this? An opportunity to go somewhere out of town on a hot date? Hardly. This was Nixon. 'I don't mind it. Jumbos leave me cold but they get me where I want to go in a hurry.'

'Small planes, as in a four-seater.' He was relaxing now, his airways back to normal speed. 'As in a scenic flight around Milford Sound.'

'You're kidding, right?' She'd grown up here and not once had she flown around the area just to look down on her home town. Her blood began to hum with anticipation. This could be fun. Especially if Nixon was part of the package. Hey, Nixon was a package—a sexy one. *Stop it.*

'Why would I be joking?'

'The smallest flying machine I've been in was a Robinson helicopter for my twentieth birthday and that was in the Abel Tasman National Park. I've never flown in a small, fixed-wing plane.' Judging by the determination in his stance, he was definitely serious. 'I'd love to go.'

'I'll swing by to pick you up at eight tomorrow. I've checked the weather and it looks superb.'

'No bumps.' The hum was raising its tempo, her blood no longer sluggish, her limbs tightening back to normal. Nixon had asked her to go flying with him. As if they were used to doing things together out of work hours. She could get used to this. 'Do I need to bring anything other than my phone for photos?'

'A light jacket. It will be cooler around the mountains. Those bumps? You're not a nervous flyer, are you?'

'Nope.'

Nixon stepped back. 'I'll see you then. Shame Rosie can't join us.'

'Yes, she'd have loved it.' But Emma would be happy having Nixon to herself for a few hours.

'Emma? What are you doing later since you're not picking up Rosie?'

'Going for a power walk along the lake.' Instant decision. Didn't want to sound completely pathetic with nothing to do this afternoon as well as tomorrow. Anyway, it was time to start getting a little bit fit again. 'Less emphasis on the power and more on the walk,' she added for clarity. Couldn't have him thinking she'd be doing something close to a run.

'Want some company?'

'Yes.' It came out before she could change her mind.

His gorgeous mouth twitched. 'Meet you about three-thirty at Steamer Wharf?'

'Sounds good.' She turned the ignition, keen to get away before he realised what he'd suggested. What just happened? Taking her flying tomorrow was amazing, and now he was joining her for a walk. After their disagreement at the park, she'd never expected he'd want to spend time alone with her again. Did that mean she was forgiven her deep and personal questions? Or he'd come to realise he'd overreacted and was trying to apologise without saying the sorry word? Guys did struggle with that.

Funny, but she didn't quite trust this alien sense of anticipation for some fun, was almost waiting for it to crash and burn. A shiver rattled through her. Dumb thing to think when she was going flying tomorrow.

'Let go the past,' commented Abbie when Emma barrelled through her open door minutes later to tell her her news.

'I thought I had.' Not completely, as it happened. 'But I know I want to.'

'Thoughts from then are bound to pop up when you start dating again. But shove them away, forget it all. Seriously, that's the way forward. Chin up, game face on, and go have a blast.' One look and Abbie had understood her confusion.

'Who said anything about a date?'

'Didn't we have this conversation a while back? Only it was you saying it about me and Callum.'

Emma felt her mouth drop. 'True, but—'

Abbie grinned. 'But it's different because it's you and Nixon and neither of you wants a relationship. I get that. So go have time with your boss and enjoy yourself.' She held her arms out for a hug. 'It really is that simple, Bestie. I know cos it worked for me.'

'Only after heartache,' Emma added as she succumbed to the hug.

'Good things are worth waiting for, and you, my friend, have been waiting a darned long time.' Abbie dropped her arms as Grace's cry reached them from down the hall. 'Someone's extra hungry today. You had lunch yet?'

'No. What've you got?'

'Bread and cheese. Creating delectable meals seems to have gone out the window. But it is fresh bread from the bakery.'

'I'll put sandwiches together while you satisfy Grace.' And by the time she'd slapped some bread and cheese together, hopefully her boobs would have returned to quiet, not this aching throb going on from the moment she heard the first cry. At least they'd had a morning off from the aches that still blasted her intermittently. Not a huge change in that since the birth, but it had to be coming soon. Fingers crossed.

Emma stretched her legs out on Abbie's couch and yawned. 'Why did I say I was going for a walk? I can hardly keep my eyes open.' She'd spent the afternoon with her friend, chilling out, having baby cuddles and handing Grace back with no difficulty. Emma didn't for a moment believe she was out of the woods, she knew there were still plenty of difficult moments ahead, but this time had helped.

'So, are you going to phone and cancel?'

Emma fixed her friend with a glare. 'As if.'

'Then move your butt, girl. You're wasting minutes you should be using to drag your running gear on and redo your make-up before driving into town early so you're not late for your not date.'

'See ya.' Emma leapt up, and instantly regretted the

hurried movement. 'Ouch.' She rubbed her stomach before rushing out and across to her apartment where she rammed the key in the door lock, or tried to. She missed and had to slow down.

Abbie's laughter followed her inside and down the hall to her bedroom where she tugged a drawer open so fast it came right out and hit the floor with a thud. Snatching up her running pants, she squeezed into them before searching for a loose tee shirt. No way could she wear her fitted sports top yet. Boobs and tummy too big. A complete refresh of make-up before snatching up shoes, phone, keys, a cash card in case they went for a drink afterwards. Expecting too much? Probably, but in for a walk, in for a drink. And if not, then she'd buy a takeaway to eat at home later. On her own.

Emma was doing light stretches when Nixon walked onto Steamer Wharf, and he had to pause. Sports pants fitted snug around her curvy butt, and when she leaned over to touch her toes the baggy shirt rose above her waist to expose creamy skin on her back.

*Zap.* A heat ray got him. In places he'd prefer not to acknowledge. Not that he denied his masculinity, but this was Emma. Emma as in friend, nurse, mother, and surrogate mother.

The oath he uttered was for his ears only. Who was he fooling here? The woman in front of him with her amazing body that not even pregnancy had turned heavy and cumbersome had found a way into places in his heart he'd firmly believed didn't exist. She hadn't entered in one hit. No, this was Emma with her sweet nature and those fears that rocked her from time to time, with her generous heart and sadness that sometimes dulled the greenest of green eyes. She'd snuck up on him when he wasn't looking.

When he was avidly avoiding involvement might be

closer to the truth. He could still avoid that. Forewarned was supposedly forearmed.

'Hey, you joining me?' the object of his desire asked, hands now firmly on her curvy hips.

Lots of curves going on here. Curves he'd only begun noticing recently. Curves he now wanted to clasp in his hands so he could lean in for a kiss.

*Shut down, Nixon, or you're not going on any walk.*

His body was sitting up to attention, and would bring him a load of unwanted attention if he didn't haul on the brakes. 'Sure,' he managed and lifted a leg to the bollard on the edge of the wharf. Leaning over, hands stretched to his ankle, he counted to ten before releasing the tension in his muscles. In most of his muscles. Not all were playing the game.

'What kept you?' Emma had strolled closer. Too damned close. 'Couldn't find your top-of-the-range outfit?'

'Cheeky.' Twisting slightly sideways, he managed to swap legs on the bollard without presenting his dilemma. 'Why are we walking when that's obviously running get-up you're wearing?'

'Not sure the body's quite ready for a run yet.'

He'd figured, but needed a conversation filler while he got everything under control. 'You ran before you got pregnant?'

'Most days I'd go out, often with Abbie. She likes to race whoever she's with, and always wins too, damn her.' Emma swigged some water from her bottle before clipping it on her belt. 'Ready?'

No. 'As I'll ever be.' Things were settling down. Hopefully hard-paced walking would finish the job. Hard? Gulp. 'Let's go,' he growled.

It was slow going through the tourists crowding the wharf and the extended areas where cafés and bars beckoned, but once they were beyond the town centre Emma upped the paced, striding out as if nothing could hold her back.

'Take it easy. No point in overdoing the exercise when you're already knackered.' Nixon matched her step for step, pulling back on the pace in an attempt to slow her down, happy to be beside her until they hit the narrow path further out of town. 'How far are we going?'

'Sunshine Bay, maybe up the hill, down the other side and probably back to town. Not far, but I'm thinking since it's been a while I'll quickly run out of steam.' She doubted she had the energy for more. "'I'll re-evaluate when we reach the lake road again. Do you run or walk much?'

'Cycling takes up most of my spare time. I started snowboarding last winter too.'

'You like seat-of-your-pants sports.' Not a question. 'I don't understand people wanting to take huge risks all the time. Are you an adrenalin junkie?'

The second person to pull him up on this in a week. Did he need to re-evaluate his approach to life now Emma was getting under his skin? He'd have to if their friendship developed into something stronger. 'I guess, though I don't see it as risky, more a way of totally focusing on something to banish all the minutiae in my head. Being distracted by wondering who's going to fill the roster next week or did I pay the power bill is dangerous. Getting injured is the last thing I want.'

'It's your go-to place when you need a break.' Emma shot him a speculative look.

'Yes.'

'Have you always done that?'

Since he was six. 'Mostly.'

Her mouth flattened. 'Right.'

Back to Sunday and that argument without even trying. He wanted to head back to town, but he hadn't got to being head of an emergency department by being a coward. So if he wasn't one then he should be opening up to Emma, explaining a little of what made him tick. But that meant exposing his fears. If his body hadn't already quietened down from the heated moments back at the wharf it certainly would now. This was scary stuff. Something deep at the back of his mind was nagging him to let go, to see where it took him. He'd already worked out Emma would be the only person he'd even consider exposing his inner demons to—if he got brave enough.

Deep breath. One, two, three. 'I lost my parents and brother when I was a child. Doing extreme things like climbing the tallest trees in the bush backing onto my uncle's property became my way of denying the mental images of them in the plane crash that killed them. I guess I haven't stopped.' The words rushed out so fast she probably didn't hear them properly.

Emma halted, tipped her head back to stare up at him, nothing but compassion in those beautiful eyes. 'Plane crash? Jeez, Nixon, that's terrible. I mean, you were a little boy. How did you deal with that?' Nothing wrong with her hearing, then. 'Sorry, I guess you've just told me how. But it's hard to comprehend what life must've been like for you. At least you had your uncle.'

'Plus older cousins.' His tone was flat, and that guilt he got when thinking about them rose. 'Henry took me in and raised me until I left for university.' His elbow nudged her to start walking again. 'Better than being submerged in the welfare system.' *And that, Nixon Wright, is ingratitude in full colour.* 'My uncle never hesitated when the news broke, and I was well looked after.'

'But they weren't *your* family.'

'Not in the way I wanted.' He hadn't been loved. Or so he'd believed, but seeing how Emma loved her daughter without being too effusive he began wondering if he'd been wrong. She wasn't loud about her feelings for Rosie, but nor was she silent. Because she hadn't lost anyone close? Uncle Henry had lost his wife, his cousins their mother, before his sister died in the plane crash, yet never hesitated to take a lost little boy into the family. Henry would've known what he was going through. That didn't mean he could be open and loving while dealing with a load of grief and his own two distressed children. No wonder the man was closed to everyone. It had become his way of coping.

*Like mine?*

'You were afraid to love them in case they disappeared overnight.' Emma saw it clear as day.

Loving anyone *was* terrifying. What if he lost them? Just because Henry didn't profess love to all and sundry didn't mean he didn't feel it. Henry would've been grieving when he'd opened his home for his sister's terrified son. No wonder love hadn't come Nixon's way in an obvious display of affection, the way his parents had shown him. If he'd hurt his uncle and cousins by thinking they didn't care then he had a lot of ground to recover.

Now she understood the determination and despair in Nixon's eyes when he'd worked on the little boy's mother in the car accident. Emma's heart cracked open some more for the little boy who'd been Nixon. He hadn't wanted the other child to suffer for the rest of his life—as he had. He'd have done anything to keep the mother alive.

Emma kept up her power walking—very little power, she grudgingly admitted, yet her lungs were burning. They headed up the hill past the international hotel and into the housing area. If she stopped she'd give into the clawing need to wrap Nixon in a hug. A hug to show him he wasn't alone. And that might signal the end of whatever they had going on between them today. He would back away. Again.

And again. She wasn't ready to risk that. She wanted more time with him, more getting to know him.

When he was talking about losing his family, his words had been terse, biting on the pain, saying in no uncertain terms he hated discussing it and she was not to start pressing him for more. No problem on that score. Guilt tightened her muscles, her skin, for pushing him so hard last Sunday. No matter that she hadn't known what was behind his three-date rule and risky lifestyle outside work. She shouldn't have pushed him as hard as she had on Sunday. Kind of explained why he was a doctor, saving people when he hadn't been able to save his family. How did anyone cope with the sudden news that the people he loved the most were gone, that he was never going to see them again? No more hugs, kisses, laughter. As for a six-year-old comprehending it—impossible.

But Nixon *had* told her. A horrific accident had stolen so much from him. A plane crash. 'I don't understand how you're okay with flying.'

'Learning to fly was another tactic to put myself out there, face the same odds my family faced.'

'You're a pilot?' The words spluttered across her lips. 'You're flying us tomorrow?'

'Yes.' He watched her as he asked, 'That all right with you?'

'Of course. It never occurred to me.' But it made perfect sense. This was Nixon after all. 'I presumed there'd be someone else at the controls.'

'You can pull out.' He gave a strained laugh that said he'd be hurt if she did.

'What? Miss out on winging over Milford Sound? Sorry, Nixon, but you're stuck with me for tomorrow morning at least.' Longer if you're interested. She nudged him forward, walking behind him on the narrow pathway. Any excuse to check out that sexy butt and those long, muscular legs sending her heart into palpitations. Nixon was no longer just a sometimes friend, or any kind of friend, but a man she was looking at very differently. Where was that going to get her? Nowhere unless he lightened up some more with her. Or maybe it was time she showed him a little of how she felt.

Whoa. Her heart rate lifted, sending her blood zinging around her veins. Tell Nixon she cared about him? Really, really liked him? Lay her heart on the line? No. He wasn't ready to hear any of that. Was she ready for this? She wasn't sure, but it seemed she also didn't want to slip back into her box and hide away from life any more.

Now what was she going to do?

Nixon stumbled, righted himself and waited for Emma to catch up. He let her retake the lead to set the pace. No longer walking very quickly, she looked thoughtful.

His hormones liked that it was slower, giving him an opportunity to admire that sweet backside that had him in a lather far too often. He shouldn't be looking, let alone thinking about those curves. But they were meant to be appreciated. They were also a wonderful diversion from the revelation that he might've been wrong about Henry. He cringed with embarrassment. He'd held himself aloof from the only family he had. Did his uncle understand why he'd done that? His cousins? What did they feel about his attitude to their father when in fact he'd been given everything he needed to grow up into a successful man?

Instead he watched Emma, ignored the guilty ache these unasked-for questions were causing. He would deal with it in good time. Nothing he could do right this minute anyhow.

After a silent ten minutes they reached the road back at the bottom of the hill and Nixon turned towards town. Emma was tired but quite capable of seeing the challenge in doing another round. 'I'm ready for a beer.' Hopefully she didn't see through his attempt to head her off.

A light red hue coloured her cheeks, and not from excursion. Running a hand over her head, she shook her head. 'Definitely out of shape. I'm going to have to put in a lot more effort, just not for a few weeks.'

So she wasn't trying to prove a point. Got that wrong, along with lots of things about Emma. He did know there was nothing wrong with her shape. Nothing at all. 'Does that mean we'll stop for a drink when we reach the wharf?'

She looked at him over the top of her sunglasses, which had slid down her nose. 'Try stopping me.' Her tongue did a lap of her lips. 'I'm picturing a cold bottle of beer already.'

'Then let's hustle because I've got the same image.' Along with another one involving that tongue on his fevered skin.

The little pub hidden away down a back street was heaving with locals when they squeezed their way inside to the bar.

'Looks like we'll be better off out in the garden when we get these.' Emma looked around. 'Can't hear myself think in here.' Her eyes were wide with happiness.

'You don't get out often enough.'

'Tell me something I don't know.'

The wistful twinge in her voice didn't dampen her pleasure beaming out at him, making him feel oddly pleased. There'd been a moment back there on the hill when he'd have sworn Emma had been about to hug him, before she'd turned away, cutting further conversation and that maybe hug. He'd been grateful and disappointed. If she'd wound her arms around him he would not have been able to resist, would've held on tight, and a little bit more of his barricade would've cracked open. Dangerous. Gulp. To be that close to her, to let someone know his history and understand him, hell, but that would be wonderful. A release. Relief. If he had that, who knew what the future could hold?

*Getting in deeper here, Nixon.*

'You going to stand there having a conversation with yourself all night?' Emma winked over the rim of her bottle, her elbows wedged on the top of the high wooden bench they were using.

He found her a smile. 'Thought you couldn't hear a thing.'

'It's way better out here.' She swallowed a mouthful of her drink. 'You moved to Queenstown from Dunedin, right?'

He nodded. Where was this headed?

'Had you come up here very often before?'

'Of course. The mountain biking is awesome, and the skiing is right up there with the best in the country.'

'Of course,' she repeated his words with a smile. 'The adventure capital of New Zealand is a perfect playground for you. Reckon this is a permanent move or will you up stakes and move away some time? Get a job in a bigger hospital?'

It might be a question people asked each other every day, but for Nixon it felt loaded. Fraught with road bumps. 'Queenstown suits me. We get more trauma injuries per capita than anywhere else in the country and those are my specialty so why leave? But who knows? A fabulous offer might come along that I'd be stupid to turn down. Though I doubt there's too much out there I'd trade for what I've got here.'

'Not a big city guy, then?'

'Not even for holidays.'

'Damn. I always planned on going to LA and the fun park when Rosie was old enough.'

What did that have to do with him? 'Never been there, and can't say it's on my list, but then I haven't had a little girl to factor into the equation.' What would it be like to go to a theme park with Emma and her daughter? There'd be lots of laughter for one.

'What's your favourite colour?'

A laugh bubbled up and out. 'Green.' As in the colour of her eyes. 'What's yours?'

'Haven't got one.' She grinned.

'Okay, what's your favourite breakfast?'

'Pancakes with bacon, bananas and maple syrup.' One eyebrow rose. 'You?'

'The whole works: bacon, eggs, hash browns, mushrooms, et cetera. Holiday destination apart from that one for Rosie?'

'Wanaka, staying in the family beach house. Summer wouldn't be the same without going there.'

That was something he hadn't had. There'd been a rumpty little shack on the West Coast his dad went to for fishing and hunting, occasionally taking the family with him, but it had been sold when the estate was wound up and the proceeds invested for his future. 'Sounds wonderful.'

'It is. As of now you are officially invited to come and stay with my lot over the summer. Bring your bike and swim shorts, beer and an open mind, and you'll have a load of fun.'

'Seriously?' Of course it was serious. Emma didn't do things by half measures. 'Invitation accepted. I am already looking forward to it.'

*And to spending more time with you away from the hospital.*

# CHAPTER EIGHT

EMMA STARED OUT of the Aero Club window onto the air-field beyond where planes were tied down in neat rows. Past the terminal, an international flight was lining up in preparation for take-off. Beyond the airport boundary Cor-onet Peak rose into the sky, dominating the scenery with its sheer rock faces and snow-capped peaks.

Excitement made her squirm. Last night's beer and pizza had been a world away from her usual Friday night, but this was out of the park.

'Ready?' Nixon called across the room from where he and the flying instructor had been talking over weather and flight paths.

She'd tuned out minutes ago, but now they were about to go flying. Looking up at the man who was becoming more important to her by the day, she nodded. 'Are you?'

He grinned, not a tense muscle in sight. 'Always when it comes to flying.' Piloting a small plane must be his best place, his most comfortable environment. If that grin was anything to go by then she'd join him at every opportunity. It sparkled with heat, was filled with cheeky temptation, so that right about now she should be getting very afraid. Because damned if she wasn't falling into the pool that was Nixon. What lay ahead for them? Patience was usually her way—except when it came to Nixon and she wanted to rush through the tape, see where they arrived and what their future held. 'Settle down,' she warned, walking beside the man tempting her heart.

In one hand Nixon held something like a large compass, a map and a key. In his other hand he held...hers.

Did he know what he'd done? Had winding his fingers through hers been an intentional move? Or was he so focused on preparing for their flight that he'd done it without thought? Meaning that he accepted her as a part of his life in some way?

Emma kept quiet, tried not to squeeze her hand a little bit tighter to feel his strength, his long fingers between hers. She was holding hands with Nixon. Her feet danced. The sky was breathtakingly blue. The air clear and crackling. She'd got it bad.

They crossed to a plane with its wings on top. 'All the better to see the view,' Nixon explained as he checked fuel, props and wiggled the rudder, explaining everything as he went. 'Right, up you get.' He held the door open for her, his other hand on her elbow as she scrambled aboard, his fingers leaving pads of heat on her skin.

When Nixon joined her from the other side he passed over a set of headphones. 'We can talk to each other through these. Be aware that at times I'll be talking to the control tower.'

Belted up and headphones clamped around her ears, Emma watched Nixon run through pre-flight checks, talk to the tower, and then off with the brakes and the plane rolled forward. 'We're away,' she said more to herself than Nixon.

'Sure are,' he came back.

The moment they were airborne, the plane leant sideways as Nixon brought it around to head directly towards the Remarkables. 'Where are we going?' she managed in a semi-normal voice.

'We're getting out of the approach path because there's a commercial flight on finals. I'll turn as soon as the tower advises me to.'

Oh. Good. Great, even. 'Do you follow instructions the whole time?'

'No. I've filed our flight outline and before take-off I told traffic control what height I intend flying at. I'll be informed of other light aircraft within my range so that I can look out for them, otherwise I'm in charge.'

Emma laughed. 'Typical.'

'Sit back and relax. Enjoy the unfolding scenery. Drinks and meals won't be served on this flight, but we can make up for that when we get back.' Nixon listened intently to the controller and finally made a slow right-hand turn.

A small sigh of relief escaped Emma. All very well being told aiming directly for mountains was okay, but changing direction was far more encouraging. Staring out and down, she gasped. 'It's so pretty from up here.' Whenever she'd flown out of Queenstown on a commercial flight the plane had been up and gone so fast she'd never appreciated her town from above.

'We'll head to Mount Aspiring first,' Nixon told her.

'Cool.' The famous mountain peak looked colder than cool when they reached it. 'Those guys are mad.' She pointed to two climbers working their way up a ridge near the top. 'What if they fall?'

'They'd be history. Looks like they've got all the gear though. They must've set out about three this morning to be that close to the summit.'

Bonkers. 'Why risk your life for a view from the top when you can fly up here?'

'It's a calculated risk if you prepare for the worst, have the right equipment, take note of the weather and act accordingly.' Nixon flew around the mountain. 'There's a lot of fun to be had if you take adventure seriously.'

Damn but zooming around the sky in a little machine with Nixon beside her was exciting. It wouldn't take much to give into the swamping need to kiss him and share the fizz in her blood, so she worked at going with the joy and beauty of it all instead. 'This is amazing.' Right now she was going to catch a rainbow and pretend she was as carefree as she felt. Because—because maybe her dreams could come true.

'Want to have a go?'

'What? At flying?' When Nixon nodded she shivered. 'Is it safe?'

'I'm not getting out,' he teased. 'Put your hands on your controls like I'm holding mine. I've got everything covered.'

'Funny how there are two sets of everything.'

'One for the instructor and one for the pupil.'

Gripping the controls, she said, 'What next?'

'Hold the plane level by keeping the controls where they are.' Removing his hands, he watched her sitting rigid for fear of moving the controls even a fraction. Putting one hand back in place, he said, 'I'm holding lightly. To make the plane go down and faster push forward slowly, not abruptly or too far.'

Her heart in her throat, she hesitated. *Wimp.* 'Right, onto it.' *Deep breath, push forward an incy-wincy bit.* Nothing happened. More pressure and suddenly the nose of the plane was dropping. She jerked backwards, bringing the controls back to where they'd been when she'd first touched them.

Nixon laid his hand over hers, gave her a gentle squeeze, sending her heart winging into orbit. 'You're doing fine. Look, I'll show you.' When he pushed forward the plane began heading down on a slow line. 'To go up you pull back, again, not abruptly. You need to add a little more power when going upwards.'

Up they came, down they went. Up down in gentle movements until Emma started laughing with glee. 'This is awesome. I can't believe I'm flying a plane.'

'Next you'll be taking lessons and getting your own licence.' Nixon high fived her. 'Right, I'm taking over now.'

Relinquishing the controls meant letting go of a different life, an opportunity to do something for herself. A glimpse into a world of adventure she'd never experienced or believed she needed. 'No matter what, I'm still a mother and a nurse with all the necessary commitments. Nothing can change that.'

'You can be whatever you choose if you want it enough,' Nixon said.

*Did I say that out loud? Must've.*

'You think it's that easy?' Then why wasn't he letting go of his issues, becoming a man with love in his life? *Gulp. I didn't say* that *out loud, did I?*

'No, I don't. Just quoting someone who probably never had a problem in his whole sorry life.' Nixon was still smiling, telling her to keep having fun, because this was one of those special days that didn't happen often.

She leaned forward to peer over the nose of the plane. 'Is that Milford?' There was a long fiord with an airstrip and a few buildings at one end. Planes were landing continuously, no doubt full of eager tourists.

'Sure is. We'll stay away from the airstrip. Too many other planes for my liking.'

That was another reason she liked Nixon. He might do adventure but he didn't take risks with her or anyone else. Or probably himself. She certainly hoped not. She wanted him around for a long time to come. 'So we go up the Sound?'

'Up the right side and back down the left. We don't fly through the middle for safety purposes. I need room to turn the plane around in the unlikely event something goes wrong.'

Her tummy didn't tighten when he said that. She was confident in her pilot, and having the best day of her life. Recent life anyway. Putting her phone to the window she clicked photo after photo. 'I think I'm going overboard but who knows when I'll ever get another chance?'

'There'd be endless opportunities if you learnt to fly.'

'No, thanks. As much as I'm loving this, if I had spare money I'd rent a block of land and have horses. But I'm saving to buy a house, so any spare dosh gets put away. Out of sight, out of spending danger.'

'Not staying in the apartment for ever?' Nixon swooped the plane around in a circle to face the way they'd come.

'Owning my own place has always been a dream since I had Rosie. I grew up in that house out in Gibbston Valley. Dad farmed cattle then. All the special memories from my childhood are to do with there and I want that for Rosie somewhere down the track. Though what I'll be able to afford will be on a much smaller scale and not in such a fabulous location.'

'It'll be a start.'

'Exactly.'

She took more photos, settled back in the seat and breathed in warm, kerosene-laden air and smiled with happiness.

Nixon grinned. 'You are enjoying this, aren't you?'

'Oh, yeah.'

'Hate to tell you but we're heading home. The plane's booked by someone else at eleven and I need to refuel.'

'I'm fine with that.' The rest of the day was going to be tame after this. The rest of her life if Nixon wasn't starting to feel the same way about her. Since he'd brought her up here anything was possible. Wasn't it?

'Want another crack at flying?'

'Can I?' Not waiting for an answer, Emma sat up straighter. 'Can I try turning?'

'Wait 'til we're well away from Milford.' Nixon was scanning the sky in front of them, out of the side windows and then above as much as he could see.

'You do that a lot.'

'First lesson in flying: be on the watch for other planes. Don't rely on other pilots or air traffic control to tell you who's in your space.' He glanced at the control panel, then at the wings. 'Straight and level. You're onto it.'

Pride filled her. Anyone could do this, but she was doing it and that felt special.

'Let's try a turn. Move the control gently to the left. Again, nothing abrupt. Too sharp and too far and you'll flip us over on our back.'

'Yikes.' Emma let the controls go, suddenly terrified at how easily this could turn to catastrophe.

Nixon's hands were instantly in charge of his controls. 'Steady.'

'You frightened me.'

'Good. You need to be wary all the time.'

'Handing back to you,' she told him. 'I prefer to relax and enjoy my flight.'

'Emma Hayes, I don't believe you're chickening out that easily. Not the strong, brave woman of these past few weeks.'

Heat blasted her cheeks at the compliment, but it was nothing compared to the heat between them. Her hands seemed to reach for the controls of their own volition. 'Talk me through the turn.'

His low, measured voice instructed her as required, allowing time for her response while watching dials, wings, the nose, her. His calm approach gave her confidence.

Concentrating harder than she'd ever done for anything else, she turned the plane to the left, and kept turning because Nixon didn't tell her to straighten up. She held her breath, took a quick glance out of the window to see the land below moving in a circle. 'Ready to straighten any time you tell me.' Thump, thud. Her heart was leaping in its cage; excited, happy.

'A few more degrees and we'll be back on line.'

'I'm doing a complete circle?' How cool was that? Dealing with a cardiac arrest was going to seem tame after this.

'Watch that the speed doesn't pick up when you straighten. Keep the wings level. That's it. You're a natural.' Nixon slapped his hand on his thigh, his fingers tapping a soundless tune.

She wished it were her thigh those strong fingers were resting on. Her muscles tightened anyway, and her skin prickled with need as though he were touching her. If only she could let go of the controls to place a hand over his. Laughter bubbled up and out of her throat, filling the small cabin. 'This is awesome. Thank you so much for bringing me up here. It's the best time I've had in for ever.' She'd left her problems on the ground and was having unfettered fun with a man she couldn't get enough of. No wonder her heart was singing.

'We'll do it again.'

Truly? She couldn't wait. 'I'll hold you to that.'

His laughter died away as a thoughtful expression expanded across his face.

Emma waited to hear whatever was going on in his mind, but he remained silent. 'It's okay, I understand if you don't get the chance. I'm usually fairly busy at the weekends too.'

'Stop it. I can't wait to take you up again.' His smile melted her. 'I haven't had a day like this, ever. You make me happy, Em.' He swallowed hard, stared outside for a moment, then focused on flying, taking over the controls and checking everything essential to a safe landing. Pressing the talk button, he spoke to Queenstown Air Traffic Control. 'Bravo Juliet Foxtrot on approach, three kilometres out, two thousand feet and descending.'

'Bravo Juliet Foxtrot, cleared for landing, out.'

'Cleared for landing,' Nixon repeated back before glancing across to her. 'You ready?'

She nodded, and watched the ground slowly come up to meet them at a steady rate. The touchdown was so soft it was as though they were still above the ground. Taxiing back to the aero club went too fast, and suddenly they were there, the prop slowing, stopping, and Nixon was pushing his door open, fresh air infiltrating the cabin and diluting the heat, the smells, the excitement.

'Welcome back to earth.' He smiled softly, again wakening her in places she hadn't known were still alive.

'I can't thank you enough.' But she was going to try. The time had come to move this forward to a whole new level, to express the kiss that had been building up since take-off. All or nothing. And nothing was no longer an option.

Unclicking her seat belt, Emma leaned over the gap between them, her hands on his upper arms, her lips seeking his. Pressing her mouth to his, she breathed deeply, gathered in his man scent, his heat, his vitality, and kissed him with everything she had.

Nixon stilled, sat tight under her onslaught.

Unable to help herself, Emma kept kissing him, her tongue beginning to explore his mouth. He tasted better than she'd imagined.

He moved closer, took over the kiss, his lips savouring hers, his tongue dancing with hers. His arms wound around her, drew her as close as possible in the awkward space they shared. The kiss moved to a depth she'd never experienced before. Nixon tasted of mint and heat and male. Under her hands his muscles were tight, strong, and knocking her heart out of shape. *Her* muscles were liquid as they pinged with heat.

Then she was set back, those wondrous lips gone, her mouth destitute.

'Sorry, Emma. I shouldn't have done that.'

'You didn't start it. I did.'

Not that she'd put any thought into it—it had just felt so natural, so right.

'I shouldn't have continued kissing you back.' His hands gripped the now useless controls in front of him.

'Fine.' If he needed space he'd get it. Using her elbow, she shoved her door wide and dropped to the ground, slammed the door shut and strode across the grass to the four-wheel drive to wait until Nixon was ready to take her home.

She was glad she'd kissed him, and stopping had been out of the question. Damn but could he kiss. Her toes were still curled and her blood hadn't returned to a normal pace. Might never. As for her heart—messy. Like putty, it had been moulded into a new shape far too easily. Now she had to find a way to straighten it out so she could face Nixon and not go into emotional overload, or do something more embarrassing than kiss him. What could be more embarrassing than that? Ah, well, there was always…

Nixon was taking his time topping up the fuel. That long body stretched across the front of the plane as he held the nozzle in place reminding her how he'd walked beside her yesterday as they'd headed up the hill in Sunshine Bay. Long, confident strides as if he were on the prowl, sexy as all be it, stirring her deep down whenever she'd glanced at him. No wonder she'd kissed him. She'd been buzzing all morning. It had had to come out somehow and what better way than in a kiss? She hadn't known a kiss could lift the lid off so many banked-down emotions.

Behind her the locks on his vehicle pinged as he headed

over. Climbing in, she waited to be driven home, probably in laden silence that said they were back to where they'd been after their last disagreement in the park.

The four-wheel drive rocked as he climbed in, then the engine roared to life and they were heading back to town.

Emma wanted to talk to him, about anything, except that kiss. She would not apologise when it had turned out to be the best kiss of her life. 'What are you doing this afternoon?' she asked, her voice a bit squeaky and high.

'Em.' He slowed at an intersection, turned onto the main road. 'Don't get mad at me, but we can't do this. It's not that I didn't like kissing you, it's that we cannot get involved.'

He liked kissing her. Not all was lost. 'Because we work together?' That would be a ridiculous reason. 'Or because you won't give us a chance?' That would be tricky but with patience and need on both sides they could work it out.

'You're not ready.'

That could be true, and it could be totally wrong. 'What makes you think that?'

'Recently you had a baby for someone else and are still coming to grips with all the emotions involved. You can't really know what you want yet.'

Her mouth dropped open as anger flared. She forced it away. Nixon deserved her truth. All of it. 'You're right. And you're wrong. My emotions are extreme at the moment but they run true. I miss Grace in my arms even though she's not mine. My body wants her while my head and heart are working to let her go.' Her hands were clenched on her thighs and didn't relax when Nixon briefly covered them with his and gave her a squeeze. 'As for us, I have no idea where or how far we're headed. I only know...' she loaded her voice with honesty '... I want to find out. To do that I'm prepared to take some chances.' Then a little imp got hold of her tongue. 'For the record, I kissed you, I didn't propose.' *Careful. That's enough.*

Nixon braked sharply for a red light, his fingers tapping in an annoying way on the steering wheel. 'I still think it's too soon for you.'

'I think you're using me as an excuse not to let go and have some fun for a change,' she dragged out over a mouthful of disappointment.

'You might be right, to a point.' Green light, and he pulled away. 'I don't want a relationship that I can't walk away from at any moment. I told you what happened to my family and the result is I'm ultra-cautious about getting close to anyone. I could hurt you, Em, and that's not happening.'

More than honest. The lack of hope was obvious. She turned to see him clearly. 'When I kissed you I wasn't asking for a lifelong commitment. It happened. I'd had a wonderful time with you and I was buzzing. It happened,' she repeated, suddenly at a loss for words. Sensible ones anyway.

'Tell me, do you want more children?' he asked.

'Yes, one day, with the right man.'

'Is this a new thing, or have you felt like that for a long time?'

*I see where you're going with this.* 'For the past nine months I've been focused on having Abbie's baby, and doing it without breaking my heart or hers. I did that, and there are no regrets.'

Nixon turned his head her way and started to say something.

'Wait. I haven't finished. What the pregnancy's done is wake up my maternal needs and, yes, one day I do want more children, a family unit with a man, not only Rosie and me. She needs siblings and a dad too. The only new thing is I'm admitting it.'

*I want to love a man, to be loved. To share a home, a life with him.*

But now she'd well and truly scared Nixon off—if he'd even been at the starter's block, and with his hang-ups that was unlikely. 'Out-of-whack emotions and all, it's time to start living in a way I haven't for years. My life is no longer on hold.' That was enough. She'd raved on too much.

'Good for you.' He was silent after that, and for once she accepted it was Nixon's way of dealing with a load of information.

She'd put herself out there; better he think it through than make an impulsive decision that he later regretted. They were close to town now. Just ahead was the café she frequented when she had time for coffee and cake. 'Drop me off here. There's something I need to get for Rosie.'

He pulled into the kerb. 'We've done it again, finished a fun time with disagreement.'

*Our way of putting up the shutters?*

Was she also a scaredy-cat? Afraid to grab what she wanted and run with it, take a risk with her heart? But she'd initiated that kiss. That was a risk. Or would've been if she'd actually considered what she was doing before she did it. Was she really ready for a relationship? Had the past finally gone? Just because she rarely had the nightmares any more, did that mean she was free to start over? Would she be able to relate to Nixon without looking over her shoulder?

Out of the four-wheel drive, she leaned in the door to eyeball Nixon. 'Not a disagreement, more like we're testing each other, digging for information and feelings. We're new at this. If I've upset you then I'm sorry. Thank you again for an amazing experience. I'll see you on Monday, and we won't go round with long faces.' Where did all this come from? She didn't do strong and forceful. Except finally she was done with meek and mild. Look where that had got her in the past. 'Please,' she added softly, far more like her.

'It's a deal.'

The best she was going to get today. 'See you.' She closed the door softly, not wanting to put him on edge again. Ducking around a group of German tourists, she headed for the book shop and a present for Rosie to take to the street Christmas party tomorrow. Might even grab that coffee and cake for herself. Would not think about a certain man and how well he kissed. No, damn it. Every sweet, hot, delicious moment and sensation was right there at the front of her mind. Why did he have to be so good when he wasn't going to follow up with another one?

# CHAPTER NINE

'SOMEONE TO SEE YOU.' Abbie nudged her none too gently.

Emma looked around the throng of neighbours filling the front lawns of adjoining properties where they lived for the street Christmas party, not seeing anyone wanting her in particular.

'Talking to Callum. Tall, dark hair, not a street resident.'

Nixon. Her heart began its now familiar thumping. 'What's he doing here?'

'Umm.' Abbie scratched her chin. 'Could he be here to see my neighbour?'

'I guess.' Yesterday he'd said he'd see her Monday, not today. Had he missed her as much as she him?

'Grab him.' As Emma began to shake her head her nagging friend grinned wickedly. 'You know you want to.'

She sure did. Could be he liked random kisses after all. 'You don't know what you're suggesting.' Because she didn't believe she could keep her hands to herself around Nixon any more. Her gazed drifted to Rosie playing soccer with the other youngsters.

'I've got her.' Abbie nudged again. 'She'll be fine.'

She'd go to get away from that annoying elbow if nothing else. Moving fast, but not quick enough to look desperate, she headed towards Nixon, caught up with him as he turned in her direction. 'This is a surprise.'

'A good one, I hope.'

He wasn't sure of his welcome? Emma slipped an arm through his. 'I'm thrilled you came. Hope you're not put off by the crowd.'

'Not at all.' Nixon tossed his keys up and down, up and down, his eyes mostly focused on her, big thinking going on behind that gaze. 'I dropped by for a coffee, and to see if you needed a hand getting a tree to decorate.'

So he wasn't avoiding the kiss. Or her spiel about where she was at now. 'All done. Come and join in.'

He hesitated. 'We get offside with each other too easily.'

'Then we get on just fine again.'

'Which suggests we both have defining lines we're not prepared to step over.' Yet. Maybe never. Or possibly sometime in the future. One thing abundantly clear was she wanted to find out, to explore whatever it was between them that had her blood thickening and hope expanding in her chest.

He shoved the keys into his back pocket, took her hand in his as they started walking back to where Abbie sat with Grace. 'What's with the party?'

'Christmas. It's an annual event. We have a barbecue and the kids get presents after their game of soccer. It brings the street together.' The whole of December was about Christmas functions. 'Rosie is excited beyond reason, especially now she's got a tree. Every morning she asks if Santa's coming today. I'll almost be glad when it's over. Almost.'

'I can picture her on Christmas morning. There'll be no holding her back.' But it was her Nixon was gazing at, his eyes bright. His smile sent ripples of desire caressing her in places that hadn't been touched in ages. So that kiss hadn't been a failure. It had ramped things up, and she wanted to do it again. As she had time and again throughout the sleepless night.

'Is Rosie playing soccer?'

'You have to ask?' Emma relaxed into his side, holding her breath until he stayed with her, didn't step away.

'Not really.' His full-wattage smile further lit up her insides, and sent another twist of desire curling through her body and downward to that special place. 'About yesterday…'

She held her breath.

'I had a lot of fun. I'm hoping we can have some more.'

'You're on, starting now. There's cold beer in the chilly bins.'

'Way to a man's heart.'

'Cheapskate.'

His arm tensed as he drew a sharp breath. 'Just so you know, that kiss was out of this world. I pulled back because I was losing control and I hate that more than just about anything.'

Best answer yet to all the questions buzzing in her head. They might be all over the place but she'd take this as a step forward, another kink in his armoury ironed out. They would be having more fun together. 'Let's party.'

'Nixon,' shrieked Rosie as she looked up from dribbling the ball towards the goalposts made of cardboard boxes, immediately losing concentration and the ball to the boy running beside her. 'You came.'

'Yes, kiddo, I did.'

'You can be my daddy partner.'

Emma froze. Awkward. The man would be gone any second. She glanced at him from under lowered eyebrows. Saw him jerk, then shrug.

'Okay. What do you want me to do?'

Pardon? This was Nixon? The man who'd pulled away from that kiss as if he'd disturbed a nest of angry wasps? Her eyebrows rose as she studied him. Yep, definitely the man she'd fantasised about all night.

'Get the ball and give it to me,' Rosie instructed, jumping up and down with glee.

*Don't let my girl down, please.*

Despite what he'd just said, he'd soon realise he'd had a brain fade and forgotten he didn't do personal. Emma's lungs started aching with the breath stalled in there. Forcing it out, she aimed for normal—if normal meant racing blood, thumping heart and disbelief as he said to her, 'Put a hold on the beer.' Then he jogged across to the kids and men—fathers—to join Rosie.

'She's too damned sassy for a kid her age,' Emma muttered as she rejoined Abbie, who hadn't missed a word of that exchange.

'Nixon looks relaxed about it all.' Abbie grinned her infuriating grin.

'Since Grace was born you've become this annoying smug—yes, *smug*—person. Well, can it. Bring back my old friend who understood where I was at in my life and left me to get on with it quietly.' Emma wheezed out the last sentence as lack of oxygen from not breathing throughout that tirade caught up with her.

Abbie laughed. And laughed. When she finally got some control she managed to splutter, 'Now I know how rattled you are.'

'I am not,' Emma ground through her teeth. She hadn't been, but she wondered if she was expecting too much. She shook off that though—now was the time to leap in and have some fun, maybe find love while she was at it. 'Not rattled, bewildered.' She held her hand up. 'No words of wisdom, please. I'm going to work this out my way.' Hopefully that would encompass another of those stupendous kisses. At least one.

'Here, get this into you.' Callum handed her a beer. 'Since I've suddenly been replaced as—' he flicked his fingers in the air '—quote, "daddy partner", I'll be the drinks waiter.'

He could stop laughing and all. Emma grabbed the beer and gratefully tipped a mouthful down her dry throat. Then nearly choked when Nixon looked across at her with such a smile of delight on his face as Rosie cheered loudly over a goal they'd scored. 'He's enjoying himself,' she muttered.

'What can I say?' Abbie gloated. Then twenty minutes later she said, 'Get that man a beer, Callum. The game's finished.'

Rosie was trotting alongside Nixon trying to keep up with his long stride, her hand in his. 'Mummy, did you see that? Nixon helped me kick a goal.'

'Clever clogs. You played really well.' Emma smoothed errant curls off her daughter's forehead and leaned down to kiss her cheek, whispering, 'Did you thank Nixon for playing with you?'

'Thank you, Nixon, for playing with me.' Rosie was jumping up and down between her and Nixon. 'I'm going to get a present, I'm going to get a present.'

Emma slapped a hand over her ear nearest that explosion, but too late. The sound reverberated through her head. 'Jeez, Rosie, down a decibel or three, if you can.'

'What's a decibel?'

Nixon chortled. 'I think your mother is saying you shout too loudly.'

'That's how I make her hear me.' Rosie had an answer for everything since starting school.

'Go on, join the other kids. The presents will be given out shortly.' Emma patted her bottom.

'Where's Santa?' Rosie's face fell. 'How will I get a present if he's not here?'

'You won't miss out, my girl. Have I created a spoilt little monster by any chance?' she asked the others.

'It's Christmas. This is what kids are like,' Abbie reassured her.

'Did you get her a muzzle by any chance?' Nixon asked.

She nodded. 'A permanent one.' Somehow she'd stepped closer to Nixon, could *feel* him beside her without touching him. As if they were a couple—an in-tune couple, not a hit-and-miss pair of messed-up characters. A permanent kind of life. Oh, hell, what was she thinking? 'The barbecues are being cranked up. You'll stay?'

*Don't say no, please don't say no...*

'Love to, but shouldn't I have contributed something?'

'There's enough food to feed twice this many people, and I brought some beer so you're all good. Anyway, you took me flying. Should I have paid half the plane rental?' she asked sharply. It hadn't occurred to her to offer when her mind had been on other things. 'I never thought.'

'I invited you to join me. I didn't expect you to pay. The only stipulation was to have a great time, and you did that.'

Gazing at Nixon, she told him truthfully, 'I certainly did. Way beyond my expectations.' So was that kiss. 'It gripped me. I felt I'd left everything on the ground for an hour.'

'That's how I feel most times.' Back to smiling. Not that he'd really stopped since he'd arrived. 'There's a freedom up there like no other, away from people, except the ones yabbering in your ear from air traffic control.'

'No white lines and pedestrian crossings.'

'Sure you don't want to take it up?'

'Yes. I don't do much for me what with Rosie and work, but it's time I found something to get passionate about. Holding those controls gave me confidence and nudged me into thinking about a whole raft of things I might like to take up, but I keep coming back to owning my own horse one day. If that sounds like mumbo jumbo it's because I spent so long getting over the past I forgot about the future.'

*And you, Dr Wright, are shaking me up something shocking. Exhilarating even.*

'We'll go up soon, take Rosie with us.'

'Yes, please.' Bring it on. The flying. And Nixon time.

How long before kisses weren't going to be enough?

*Settle, Emma. Getting ahead of yourself here. Until two weeks ago you weren't interested in any guy, or having fun and kisses and—and sex.*

Whoa. Sex? It did follow on from the kind of deep and meaningful kiss they'd shared. But sex—with Nixon? Why not? With all the aches her body had going on? She shuddered. Maybe not.

'I'll go help Callum at those barbecues.' Nixon sauntered off.

'He looks like he belongs here,' Abbie muttered.

'Shouldn't you be watching Grace?' Emma growled.

'Just saying.'

Emma swallowed a laugh. 'Can I have a hold?' She reached out for Grace, who was staring up at her. 'Hey, gorgeous. How're you doing?' Snuggle, snuggle. Sigh.

'That sounded like a wish.' Abbie was watching her, no longer smiling or teasing, now in concerned-friend mode.

'Not for Grace, in case you're worried.' Yes, holding Grace still cranked up the hormones something terrible but it had got easier over the past few days. The gaps between feeling lost and needy for this baby were stretching longer and occurring less frequently. No, this feeling going on inside her involved Nixon and her own family. 'If anything's come of having Grace it's that I'm missing out on so much. Would it be greedy to want another baby? No, let me rephrase that. A family. The whole shebang. Loving man, more children.'

'What's greedy about that? It's what most of us want eventually, after we get the crazy stuff out of our systems. This anything to do with Nixon?'

'Lots.' There. She'd admitted it out loud. To the one person who'd treat it with the care it deserved. 'But I'm scared. It doesn't help that Nixon's not ready and nothing's going to happen.'

'You could try enjoying the moments. One step at a time. Says the woman who was never going to find love again, and *kapow*!'

A sense of well-being encompassed Emma. Excitement, caution, need, independence. Every emotion in the book rolled through her without tipping her sideways, instead leaving her with an easy acceptance.

'Very profound.' Abbie chuckled. 'We're two mature, life-damaged women and we've arrived at that? I like it. What will be tonight is you and Nixon sharing over-cooked steak and sausages off the barbecue along with soggy coleslaw made by our favourite elderly neighbour and baked spuds in tinfoil still hard in the middle. But, hey, you won't notice, because you've hardly noticed a thing since he turned up. Then you'll take Rosie home, tuck her in bed, and snog Nixon senseless. How's that?'

Perfect. 'Don't expect me to report in with a running commentary.' She handed Grace back to her mother with only a tiny backward glance. 'Better go see how Rosie is doing. I got her a pogo stick for her present.'

Seems Nixon had beaten her to helping Rosie. He was holding the stick and Rosie's arm as she tried to bounce along the path. 'Don't lift your feet off the step,' he instructed. 'That's it. Now lift your legs and the stick at the same time. Like this.' Without letting go of Rosie he did a good impersonation of bouncing on a stick when he didn't have one.

Rosie wobbled on the stick, concentrating fiercely, then bounced. A tiny bounce, but it was real.

'Go, girl,' Emma encouraged. 'Do it again. Yes, awesome.'

Nixon walked alongside Rosie, keeping her steady as she got the hang of the motion.

Then, 'Let go, Nixon. I can do it on my own.'

'Yes, ma'am.' But he kept his hands close, ready to catch her if—when it all turned to custard. After three bounces. 'Got you.'

He'd make a good dad for that baby she wanted. Bumps lifted on her skin. Far too soon, Emma. 'Okay, you two, come and get some dinner.' She couldn't watch any more now that idea had struck. Nixon helping Rosie with her kite last weekend had started the hope rising, and today was lifting it to a whole new level. But Nixon would say he wasn't used to playing with kids, and that he had a lot to learn. 'You're a natural,' she told him over burnt sausages and well-done steak.

'At what?' he asked before loading dressing-laden salad into his mouth.

'Being social.' No need to scare the pants off him. Now there was a thought. Her eyes did a quick cruise over his butt. A brilliant thought. Tempting. And would certainly put the kibosh on being friends afterwards.

Rosie was exhausted after her exciting afternoon and went to bed unexpectedly early without a whimper. 'Goodnight, sweetheart.'

'I want Nixon to tuck me in.'

*Take a back seat, Mummy.*

'Nixon, you're required.'

He strolled into Rosie's bedroom, taking up all the space, and leaned over the bed. 'Hey, sport, you did good on that pogo stick. And you got a soccer goal.'

'I'm clever, aren't I?' Rosie gave an impish grin and held out her hand to high five.

'Very clever. But it's time you went to sleep. You've got school tomorrow.'

Emma choked. Nixon sounded like a regular dad. He'd probably got it from his uncle speaking to him as a child. The number of times she said things to Rosie, told her off for a misdemeanour or praised her, in the exact same words and tone as her mother had used with her had her expecting to find her mum was sitting on her shoulder putting the words in her mouth.

Moving to the other side of the bed, she bent down and kissed her gorgeous girl. 'Goodnight, darling. Sleep tight, make sure the bedbugs don't bite.'

'There're no bugs in my bed.' Rosie shuffled further down the bed, tucking the blanket around her cute little face. 'Night, Mummy...night, Nixon.' Then, 'Mummy, is Santa coming tomorrow?'

'Not for some more days.'

'He's taking for ever,' Rosie sighed. 'I can't wait that long.'

'You're going to have to, my girl.'

Out in the kitchen Emma put the kettle on. 'Tea or coffee? Or there's beer if you want some.'

'Coffee, ta.' He came to stand beside her, that enticing butt parked against the edge of the bench. 'I enjoyed today.'

'Nothing wrong with a good old street party with the kids and oldies all mixed in. Abbie and I started it our first year here. Some of the older folk don't have family in the area and the busy build-up in the weeks before Christmas with parties and celebrations seemed lonely for them so we went door knocking and told everyone let's have a barbecue on the street.' Now it was an annual event.

'What I meant was I enjoyed hanging out with you and Rosie, with your friends. It was comfortable and fun, and…' he raised a hand to lift a curl off her cheek '…and perfect. I could get to wanting to do it regularly.'

*Knock me down.* 'You can join in any time you like.'

'It's that simple?' He breathed out the question.

Emma shook her head. 'It's getting to be, the more time we spend together.'

'Is that how you approach everything, Em?' His eyes locked onto hers. 'You didn't mind stepping out of your comfort zone and going flying with me. You obviously love your job and nothing seems to daunt you there. You're bringing up Rosie single-handedly for all the world like it's a breeze. But I see moments of wariness and worry clouding your eyes when you think no one's watching. I know you have trust issues, and understandably so, but are you really so at ease with me, with us?'

'Blimey. Don't hold back, will you?' He was asking things he would not answer if she reciprocated. She spooned coffee into a mug and dropped a teabag into another. 'Everyone has moments of uncertainty. I've told you some of mine. Having Grace gave me a huge jolt and got me thinking there was more out there if I'd just grab it. I've been afraid I'd get it wrong again if I ventured into the world of men and love, but suddenly I'm sick of hesitating. I want to put my toes in the water and to hell with the consequences. I've survived the past. I can survive the future.'

'You kissed me. Should I take that as a compliment?' Serious face on. Meaning?

'You're the first man I've kissed in many years.'

'Definitely a compliment.' A teasing smile appeared.

Emma dropped the teaspoon and leaned closer to him, drawn in by that smile and the intensity in his eyes, by the muscular body dwarfing her small frame, by the man scent pervading the air between them. 'You like compliments?' she whispered.

'Let me give you one.' Then his hands were on her arms,

bringing her close, his head dipping to find her mouth. His lips covered hers, possessed hers, sent need spiralling out of control to every corner of her taut body. Melting against him, she returned the kiss, gave herself to him with no barriers in the way. Nothing but them. Together. Kissing. Needing. Wanting. Complimenting each other.

'Mummy, I'm thirsty.'

Emma jerked away from Nixon, her cheeks flushed, her heart disappointed. 'The real world of a single mum.' She sighed and grabbed a glass to fill with water. 'Sorry.'

'Don't be. It's how it is. Real.'

The smile Nixon gave her took the strength from her knees, leaving her incapable of moving while she took some deep breaths. Real? Was this sensation of losing her grip on reality real? This need for love and family clawing through her? Was that real? Should she be following up or heading for the hills while she could still think?

'Don't take this the wrong way, but I should be heading home before we take this too far.' There was a load of regret behind his words negating her sense of being dumped when things were heating up. 'You have a child in the next room we have to be mindful of.'

'It's not just about us.'

'No, Em, it's not.'

How many men would've considered Rosie when wanting to get close to her mother? They'd have been focused on that kiss and heading down the hall to her bedroom if the altering shape of Nixon's jeans was anything to go by. He wanted her. Her. The woman who'd had a baby not long ago and wasn't looking slim any more. Stretching up on her toes, she caressed his chin with her lips. 'Thank you. And goodnight.' She'd just fallen even further into the pool.

# CHAPTER TEN

'THE CHOPPER CAME in as I padlocked my bike to the rack,' Nixon told Emma the next morning. He'd been watching out for her at the hospital car park, feeling like a lusty teenager any time one of his staff went past and he didn't walk in with them. But he was busting to see her face, listen to the cadence of her voice. Yeah, right, what he really wanted was a repeat of last night's kisses. Out in the car park? Got it bad, man. Then Emma arrived and he couldn't deny the happiness spreading throughout his body.

'Wonder what we're getting.' Exhaustion flattened her voice.

'Not much sleep last night?' Sleep had been elusive for him with a certain nurse bouncing around inside his skull. Watching her with Grace yesterday had settled something within him. Emma was coming to terms with what she'd done. Her bravery and strength stole his breath away and yanked at his heartstrings. She was one courageous woman. The kind of woman he could imagine spending the rest of his life with—if he found the same courage to let go of his lifelong hang-ups. How did he learn to do that? If he'd really copied Henry to becoming the man he was there were no examples to follow out of the quagmire.

'Darling daughter was up and down all night. Demanded drinks, needed the bathroom, wanted a story—

didn't happen—had to talk. Wanted Santa to visit.' Emma shivered. 'The joys of motherhood.' The soft smile she wore belied her shudders.

'Nights like that happen often?' How did she cope with work when they did?

'Sometimes she has a run of them then sleeps through ten hours for weeks on end.' Emma tried stifling a yawn, but it won out. 'I thought I'd have trouble waking her up this morning.'

Nixon's phone pinged. A quick glance, and, 'We're on. The chopper's patient is being taken into ED.' There was a spring in his step as they headed inside. Being an emergency specialist made him useful and needed. Helping people at their most vulnerable gave him huge satisfaction. Add in a weekend filled with Emma and it was surprising his feet even touched the floor.

Then he saw his patient and the gloss diminished. Trish and her husband Bill owned the greatest little bagel cart, his favourite go-to for quick, delicious food when on a bike ride. 'Trish, what brings you here?' Nixon walked beside the stretcher being pushed into the department.

Callum filled him in. 'Trish was walking her dog when she fell down the power track out at Arrowtown. We airlifted her to avoid a three kilometre hike out with the stretcher. Suspected broken ankle and sprained wrist. Obs are normal so it doesn't appear likely an event precipitated the fall.'

'Punch saw a hedgehog and took off, and I ran after him,' Trish grumped.

'Where's the dog now?' Her white and brown bitsa was a legend for lapping up attention outside Trish and Bill's cart.

'One of the ambulance crew that walked in took him out to meet up with Bill.'

'Bill's not here?' Nixon asked.

'He's coming in when he's arranged for someone to staff the cart,' Callum said before giving Nixon more medical details.

'Let's get you sorted, Trish. I'll check your ankle, but judging by the angle it's at you're headed to Radiology. We'll get pictures of that wrist too. Any other sore spots?'

Trish shook her head. 'No.'

'No headache, dizziness? Cramps? Something out of the ordinary?'

'Not a thing.'

'Hey, Trish. Heard you were here.' Emma arrived from dumping her bag in her locker and smiled at their patient. 'Came luxury class too.'

'Beats being carried out of the bush.' Then Trish's face dropped. 'If my ankle's broken I'm going to have to put it up, right?'

'Afraid so,' Nixon agreed. 'Bill will have full range of the cart for a while.'

'Don't smile about it, Doc. I'm the bagel queen, not him.'

'I wouldn't have said Bill was any kind of queen.' Emma chuckled. 'All bloke from top to toe, not that I've seen his toes, mind. Does he wear nail polish under his socks?'

'I heard that, young lady,' growled Trish's husband from behind them. 'Just as well I broke the speed limits to get here. Who knows what stories you'd make up about me given half a chance?'

'Bill, glad you're here.' Nixon nodded.

While Emma wrapped him in a hug. 'You didn't wait for Punch, then?'

'The medic said they'd drop him round at the house.'

Nixon shook his head. 'The patients those guys carry. Let's get Trish onto a bed. I'm sure Callum wants his stretcher back so he can go rescue someone else.'

'More like grab a coffee and some breakfast,' Callum

said. 'Good luck, Trish. Bill, if you need a hand with anything around the property while you're short staffed give me a call.'

'Sure will. There's a lot to be sorted before the auction next month.'

Emma stilled. 'Auction? You're not selling my favourite house?'

'Yes, lass, we are,' Bill started. 'It's getting too big for us, and neither of the lads are interested in coming back to live in Queenstown. We want a new house that doesn't need loads of upkeep and a section I can mow in five minutes not five hours.'

'Mum never said a word.' Emma's mouth drooped and the gleam in her eyes dulled. 'I have a lot of happy memories playing there with Trish and Bill's sons when I was little,' she told Nixon. 'Our families are close.'

'How many acres you got, Bill?' Nixon asked.

'Four and a bit. The house is big with five bedrooms.'

Emma's sigh was long and nostalgic. 'It's ideal for a couple with young children.' She shrugged, lifted those eyes to him. 'Need me for anything before I head to triage?'

A kiss. With some follow up! Knowing the feeling of her body in his arms, small and light, strong and hot, he had no chance of forgetting the desire she lifted in him. Yep, idiot that he was, still not a hundred per cent certain how ready Emma was, he wanted to hold her in his arms to repeat that kiss, to have a relationship with her. Which underlined how messed up he was, because relationships were what other people had, not him. 'I've got this.'

'Sure.' No tension today. But then last night had ended on a good note. A hot note.

*Forget what it felt like to have Emma's lips on yours, her body pressed close to your chest. Just forget it, okay?*

*Right now you're a doctor—with a patient waiting for your undivided attention.*

Poking his head out of the cubicle, he looked around for an available nurse, wishing Emma were free. 'Carl, in here.' Back to Trish, trying not to give her any more pain as he touched the swollen ankle. 'I'd say you've fractured some tarsal bones. I'll arrange an X-ray now. Carl, can you clean that wound on Trish's upper arm and I'll put some sutures in shortly?'

Emma returned. 'We've got a twenty-year-old tourist in the waiting room who walked in off the street after riding his bike into the back of a truck. Broken nose, teeth, shoulder injury. Concussion likely. I tried to bring him straight through but he refused to budge.'

Nixon approached the guy sitting half sprawled on the chairs, covered in blood and looking miserable. In pain and angry. 'I'm a doctor. Do you speak English?'

*'Sì,'* a girl beside him answered. 'A little.'

So why hadn't they talked to Emma? 'Come through so I can examine you.'

'Rocco trying talk to insurance,' the girl explained. 'We wait 'til he know.'

Nixon shook his head. 'You'll come now.' The financial side of things was someone else's problem. 'Rocco needs medical help, now.' If he said *now* often enough, the message might get through. The guy needed stitches on his chin and forehead at least. His left arm was held against his chest. Broken arm or problem with the shoulder? Cameron wouldn't be thrilled at getting an unexpected surgery this early in the day.

Emma brought over a wheelchair. 'You come.' She nodded at the girl. 'Jen, call me if anyone comes in.'

The receptionist nodded. 'Will do.'

With Rocco on a bed, Emma began peeling away clothes so Nixon could see the extent of the injuries.

Nixon caught a whiff of strawberry that was Emma. He wasn't usually aware of the perfumes female staff wore, but his senses were hyper alert around Emma. Saturday, crammed into the Cessna, he'd breathed that scent, heard her every breath and movement, felt the air shift around them, known her excitement when she held the controls. Ever since, he'd been fighting those senses, trying to squeeze them back in their place and denying she'd piqued his interest on every level. He'd still gone to see her even when he'd also been busy reminding himself why they shouldn't have a fling. If it was going to be a three-date thing, there was only one outing left.

In the waiting room, a poster on the wall advertised a band playing on the foreshore this Friday night. When they had a spare moment he'd ask Emma if she'd like to go. Hopefully her mother or Abbie would babysit Rosie.

So much for being friends. Friends didn't kiss each other with tongues involved. Didn't share kisses that cranked up the heat in his veins, in his groin. Kisses that knocked the air out of his lungs. Kept him awake all night, every night. Emma was the reason he felt lethargic and groggy and had to fight to concentrate on his patients.

'Doctor, put these on.' Emma winked as she held out two latex gloves.

'Thank you, Nurse.'

'You want me to collect the suture kit?' She grinned. 'You do seem a little distracted this morning.'

She was flirting with him. 'Would you please go to the cupboard by Resus and get the kit off the third shelf and bring it to me?' He grinned back. So this was what it was like to get a little closer to someone. Fun, flirty, and exciting. As long as he remembered first and foremost why he was here. 'Rocco, I am going to examine your arm and shoulder.' He looked to the young woman. 'Understand? *Comprendo?*'

*'Sì.'* She rattled off something in what sounded Italian and his patient lifted his arm.

*'Comprendo?'* Emma laughed. 'Stick to your day job, Doctor!'

'Rocco, tell me where this hurts.'

Asking Emma out would wreck the three-date rule because this wouldn't be the last time. Emma was tearing down his norms, beating the barriers to the ground, intriguing him, tempting him into an area he'd never stepped in before.

His skin lifted as a chill touched him. *Don't invite her. Find a woman who wants fun for a night and walk away in the morning without a backward glance.*

He'd done that too often; now he wanted something different, something more sincere, something with possibilities.

Wanting was one thing...actually following through was another. There'd be consequences for both of them. Was he ready? Was he not? When would the point come when he threw caution aside and leapt in? Now?

Emma slipped her new blue blouse over her head and smoothed it down her breasts. Breasts that had mostly stopped aching every time Grace cried. They were starting to resume their old shape and size. The blouse with its downward pattern added to the slimmer look. The short black skirt hugged her hips and settled at mid-thigh.

Slipping on shoes with killer heels, which would give her pain by the end of the night, she studied the result in the full-length mirror. Not bad considering she wasn't back to her figure yet. Excitement fizzed along her veins. A night out with a hot guy. A night where she could forget being a mum, and be a single woman having fun. A night that could lead to anything.

The doorbell buzzed. Old monsters tapped her brain,

tightening her stomach. Was she doing the right thing? She trusted Nixon, believed he was genuine, so, yes, right as right could be. Slinging the strap of her purse over her shoulder, Emma headed for the front door and the man who was pressing the button a second time. 'Let's go party,' she quipped as she shut the door behind her.

The atmosphere was electric when they pushed their way through the crowd to a street bar for some beer. The band was in full swing and people were laughing, dancing, and drinking. Every language in the book seemed to be in the air, tourists and locals mixing comfortably. 'I haven't been to anything like this in years,' Emma told Nixon, who held her hand firmly.

'Sleeping Beauty awakens,' he replied, those beautiful eyes twinkling.

'Don't think that makes you a prince,' she retorted around a smile.

Downtown, they strolled around the crowd's perimeter to find somewhere to sit, watch and listen. But within minutes of settling on a stone bench Emma stood up to sway in time to the music. When she tipped her head back to stare up at the sky her hair swung from side to side. A glance at Nixon showed his eyes fixed on her hair and a thrill of excitement caught her. Say what he liked, he was keen on her. 'Hey.' She held out her hand. 'Get your butt up here and show me your moves.'

His eyes widened but he was on his feet in an instant. 'You're on.'

Bleeding heck. The man had all the right moves. Those long legs were whippet-strong, his body bending and rolling, and his eyes—locked on her all the time. Blasting her with heat, drying her mouth, softening her limbs and forming warm knots in her stomach and places beyond. Winding her arms around his neck, she continued dancing. When his hands spread across the small of her back she felt secure and safe and happy and—yes, damn it, totally ready for a whole lot more than kisses.

'We've got all night,' he breathed beside her ear.

Her answer was to move her hips against him, to sway in time to the music up against his chest, teasing her nipples tight. All night. The words repeated in her head. A promise? Oh, yes. That was her interpretation and she was sticking to it.

They danced until the band took a break. Nixon asked, 'You want to find somewhere for a meal?'

The air was warm, the sky sparkling with stars. 'How about street food from one of the carts and we take it down on the foreshore?'

'Sounds good to me. We can come back to dance some more afterwards.'

She slipped her hand into his, and they queued for kebabs, just like any regular couple. Except nothing was regular for her. 'Dating could become my favourite pastime.'

'Mine too.' Nixon ran a finger down her cheek, across her lips. 'Think we can do this without falling out at the end of the night?'

'I'm over that. We get on so well I don't like it when we have a spat. So, yes, we can, we will, go home happy with each other.' Her fingers on her left hand, the one out of his sight, crossed ever so slightly. No harm in adding a dollop of good luck to the mix.

Tasty food sitting on the foreshore amidst the crowd, a buzzing atmosphere, and Nixon dancing with her. What more could a girl want? She had it all. The hours flew past in a blur of heat, yearning, sore feet from those heels, and Nixon. Nixon's smiles, his kisses, his hands on her back and her waist and her shoulders; laughter that made her forget everything but him.

Then the band was packing up and the crowd spilling deeper into the town centre where the bars were waiting.

Nixon draped an arm over her shoulders and tucked her close to him. 'Want another drink?'

'I hate admitting this but I'm ready to quit.' Nine-thirty bedtimes were her norm these days.

'I'm relieved,' he whispered. 'And I don't have Rosie to blame.' His chin grazed her cheek before his mouth covered hers.

'A couple of geriatrics, aren't we?' she said when they pulled apart.

'I didn't say the night was over. I'm just not interested in hanging around with half of Queenstown and a gazillion tourists any longer.'

The night wasn't over. Anticipation pushed aside her growing weariness. Her feet found a second life, all but skipping back to Nixon's vehicle. Then cold reality struck. He probably meant he'd have a coffee with her before heading back to his place. This was Nixon, the avoidance expert.

'Where's Rosie tonight?' he asked when he parked outside her front gate.

'At Mum's.' As in, not coming home until after breakfast. She held her breath. Should she make a move? Ask him in? But the words weren't there. She didn't know how to invite a man into her home for some loving, and was afraid of being turned down when she wanted it so badly.

Nixon got out of the four-wheel drive and came around to open her door, held her hand as she climbed down, kept hold of it all the way up the path, through the door, and along the hall to her bedroom. Not a word, not a questioning look. Confident and certain was this Nixon.

The insecurities fell away as he turned to her, took her in his arms and said, 'May I?' and kissed her thoroughly. A kiss deeper than any she'd experienced. A kiss that sparked to life all the desire and need she'd been trying to keep a lid on from the moment she'd opened her door to him earlier.

She was free, able to do what she'd wanted to do with Nixon for ages. He was giving her the opportunity and wouldn't back off.

Then that hot, tantalising mouth tugged away. 'This isn't too soon for you? It's only been a few weeks since the birth.'

It might hurt a bit, but somehow she believed that'd be lost in the heat and need and desire. 'Let's see how it goes.'

'I'll be careful.'

That was a bucket of cold water being tipped over her feverish skin. She kissed him to show she had no intention of going carefully. It must've worked because his fingers were at the buttons of her blouse, clumsily undoing them, his skin skimming hers. As soon as the buttons were dealt with she tugged the blouse off and tried to squeeze out of the tight skirt. Nixon's hands covered hers, pushed the skirt down over her butt, her thighs, to her knees, where it dropped around her feet. And then…one touch and she was quivering and tight and hot and cold. And crying for him to hurry.

'I don't want to hurt you, Em.' His fingers did some serious touching, whipping up a storm along her veins.

'You're not. You're—' She gasped around a shudder of need. 'You're— Let me touch you.'

'Wait. We've got all night.'

*Yes, but there are two of us here.* 'I won't last five seconds if you keep doing that.'

'Then I'll have to do it again.'

*You're welcome.*

As she gave into the shudders wracking her body her world spiralled out of control. She was sprawled across Nixon, his naked torso an aphrodisiac under her palms. Not that she needed one. Everything about Nixon turned her on. When had they got onto the bed? His erection pressed against her belly, his tongue now teasing her tender nipple, a tenderness she forgot as waves of need rolled through her when she'd barely recovered from the first onslaught.

Pushing up, tugging free of that exquisite mouth, she reached for him, held him, moved slowly, up and down.

'Condom,' Nixon gasped.

'Let's keep doing it this way.' It felt right, and eased her worry of being too close too soon after the birth.

'Emma,' Nixon groaned. Then he was back to arousing her, and they were together, moving as one, the pressure building. He brought her to the peak, restraining himself until she exploded, then quickly joined her.

Emma's breathing took for ever to return to normal. If that was making love then she hadn't lived. How soon could they do it again? Hell. She hadn't even got her breath back. Neither had Nixon. Her hand reached for his, her fingers interlaced with his. Hot, sweaty, strong, gentle. Now she knew what those hands had been made for. And she wanted to get to know them even more.

# CHAPTER ELEVEN

NIXON WATCHED EMMA scooping Rosie up into her arms and kissing her on both cheeks. 'Anyone would think you'd been apart for a week, not one night.' He chuckled, acknowledging the warmth and tenderness in his gut, and his heart, for both these adorable females.

Making love with Emma last night, he'd felt as if his world had finally come together for the first time since his family had left him. It had been a revelation. Emma was so generous with her loving he'd been lost for a while. Then she'd grounded him, made unspoken promises of more to come if he was prepared to reach out and take a chance. He'd gone into this thinking he'd be able to knock the monkey off his back for good, return to being friends once the mystery of Emma was exposed. He had not expected to feel smitten, to want more, to hate the idea of closing the door on what they had. Friends they might've been, but now they were so much more. They were lovers.

For now.

For longer?

For ever?

That meant accepting he'd never again be abandoned by someone he loved, or at least making the most of every day between now and when—if—that happened. Might mean accepting he had been loved all along as he grew up.

'Nixon, pick me up,' demanded Rosie. 'I want a hug.'

'What madam wants, madam shall have.' He swung the bouncing girl up against his chest, savouring the closeness, absorbing the smell of soap and cornflakes and…? 'You had chocolate for breakfast?'

'Don't tell Mummy I ate a Santa off the tree.'

'It's our secret.'

Rosie wriggled and wriggled, her small hands batting at his shoulders. 'Can we take my kite to the park?'

Nixon looked over her head to Emma, and raised an eyebrow.

'Later. Wave goodbye to Grandma, Rosie.'

'It'll have to be the waterfront. I'm on call,' Nixon said.

'Not a problem.' Emma led the way inside her apartment and dropped the newspaper Kathy had brought on the table. After filling the kettle, she flicked through the pages until she got to the real-estate section. 'Trish and Bill's place is a feature.' She read the details. 'Shame nursing's not the highest paying job in town.'

'You'd buy the place?' Nixon asked. He'd heard the longing in her voice when she'd talked with Bill in ED, but hadn't realised how much she yearned for it.

'I would if I had a family, as in more kids and a partner. And the dollars. Plenty of them, since Queenstown's some of the most expensive real estate in the country.'

A home and family of his own. A chill slid down his spine. Too soon. Just because they'd slept together didn't mean they were setting up house.

Picking up the paper, he read about the property that had captured Emma's heart. He could see how it would be a great place for youngsters to grow up, could visualise Emma and Rosie in the yard playing with a dog, those horses she yearned for in the paddocks. Hell, he even wanted to see himself fitting into the picture. Domestic bliss. Except that wasn't on his horizon. Certainly wasn't part of his plans for the future, despite the feeling of well-being today. He was getting closer, but still had a long way to go before he moved into a home with a wife and children. A very long way.

The old fears began kicking up a storm. His feet were itching to run out of the door, his heart beating a heavy tattoo—*don't go, get out of here, don't go, get out of here.*

A hand touched his upper arm. Emma stood staring up at him. 'Don't torture yourself, Nixon. I am not asking anything of you. We're doing great, no arguments, all fun and agreeability. Leave it be.'

'I'm that obvious?'

Her head bobbed. 'Afraid so.'

'That's scary in itself.' It was. Women didn't get to know him well—he made sure of it. But then he hadn't met an Emma before. He stared into her trusting eyes, his fears receding, leaving him shaken but—but okay. Ready to stay with Emma for the day. He could even return to the conversation that had tipped him sideways. 'You want to own your home.' It was most Kiwis' dream.

'That's what I'm saving for.' The kettle clicked off and she poured the boiling water over the coffee grounds.

Emma had plans, she wasn't resting on the mess of her past, even though it lurked behind her eyes when she was tired or upset. She'd dealt with her marriage in a similar manner to how she was dealing with post-partum blues. Brave, strong, and doing just fine with the occasional flare up of distress. 'You ever want any more hours in ED just tell me.'

'I am not cutting back my time with Rosie. We'll get there when we do, and meantime we're not living in a hovel.' Sniffing the coffee-scented air, she asked, 'That house you're in is yours?'

'Yes. I bought it off the guy I replaced in ED. He was heading to Wellington and wanted shot of the place fast. It's handy to work, easily accessible, and will only improve in value over the years, so I signed a contract immediately. Made moving from Dunedin a lot simpler.'

His phone pinged. 'Hold that coffee. A hang-glider has crash-landed on Bob's Peak close to the gondola building. Multiple injuries. Patient critical.' He called in. 'I'm coming in.' He'd prefer to go to the site but the paramedics would be there and they knew what they were doing.

'Come back for lunch if you're finished in time,' Emma called after him.

With a wave he leapt into his vehicle and gunned the motor. Of course the traffic was diabolical, with sightseers gaping out of windows and forgetting to drive. The locals were obvious—they were the ones with their hands on the horns. If only he could legally stick a flashing light on his roof.

For the first time, being called into work for an emergency didn't raise the adrenalin, didn't create anticipation for the injuries he'd have to deal with. Instead his heart got heavier with every kilometre he drove away from Emma. At least he had lunch with her to look forward to—if he ever got through this damned traffic. More time with Emma was imperative to his well-being, and the sense of balance coming into his life. Didn't matter what they did, as long as he was with her. Keep this up and his cycle might become rusty.

'Move it.' His palm pressed hard on the horn. 'Get out of the damned way.' A patient could die while he sat in this traffic jam. If his bike had been at the back of the four-wheel drive he'd be parking up and riding to the hospital by now. But it wasn't. He'd been too busy thinking about Emma to do anything that sensible.

Finally he was racing through the hospital, his vehicle abandoned in a tow-away area of the health department's car park. 'How far away is our man?'

'Coming down now,' Carl told him. 'Resus one's ready.' The nurse handed Nixon a scribbled note. 'The general surgeon and neurosurgeon are on standby, and surgical are contacting Cameron.'

'Thanks,' Nixon muttered, his eyes sweeping over the information. Moments later they were dealing with the worst of worst-case scenarios. Fractures, blood loss, unconsciousness, internal injuries. Everyone worked fast, fighting the impossible, agonising minute after agonising minute, slowly winning, getting their patient ready for Theatre.

'No reaction from his feet or hands,' Nixon warned Cameron when he arrived dressed in gardening clothes.

'Damage to the spinal cord. Makes sense. Those impact injuries to his femurs and ilium suggest he landed feet first.' Cameron studied the X-rays on the screen in front of them. 'First things first, starting with that liver haemorrhage. It's going to be a long day.'

Especially for the man they didn't have a name for.

'He arrived at the car park this morning, set up his hang-glider and took off, only to go splat against the mountainside,' Nixon told Emma that afternoon. 'A hang-gliding instructor thought there'd been gear failure, but that hasn't been verified yet.'

'Can't he be traced through the car reg?'

'It belongs to a woman in Christchurch who's in Auckland for the weekend.'

'In the meantime, the man is alone and suffering dreadfully.' Emma sighed.

Nixon sprawled out on the lounger on Em's deck, and begged the phone gods to keep the damned thing silent for the rest of the day. Exhaustion softened every muscle in his body. Hunger pangs cramped his gut.

'Get these into you.' Emma held out a plate with two salmon bagels and an icy bottle of water.

Placing everything on the table, he reached for Emma to pull her onto his thighs. It felt so right with her sitting there. 'Thanks for this. Coming in after a heavy time in ED to find you and sandwiches waiting is just…' his voice hitched '…just something I haven't had and it's wonderful.' Made him feel different, as if he belonged somewhere with someone. Pulling Emma close, he kissed her. It started gently, lips to lips, then deepened so that his blood stirred and desire overtook all thought processes. His hands slipped under her shirt, found those soft mounds.

Suddenly Emma pulled away, her breasts rising and falling rapidly. 'We can't. Rosie's in the back yard.'

Reality check. Yet while it meant tugging the brakes on his need, Rosie's presence didn't bother him. She was part of the deal. What deal? They hadn't come to any arrangement. Did he want to? What did he want from Emma? A meal? A date and sex occasionally? Or to share a beer on the deck?

*Getting too clinical here, man.*

It went to show how little experience of dating he had. In the past when he'd taken a woman out there was no comeback, no questions about where they were headed, no child to interrupt a hot kiss that was heading down the hall to the bedroom. This was a whole new deal.

Liking it?

*Oh, yeah.*

'You'd better stay for dinner.' Emma stood up. 'Hope you like chicken burgers. Saturday night dinners are Rosie's choice.'

'I'd eat anything if it means I get to stay.'

Her grin turned wicked. 'I'll see what's in my diary.'

* * *

The next week was a mix of excitement and exhaustion for Emma. While the post-birth tiredness had dissipated over the week since they'd first made love, having Nixon here kept her on high alert. Tonight he hadn't left after dinner, instead had taken her hand and led her to her bedroom to make love, not once but twice throughout the night. 'Thank goodness Christmas is almost here,' she murmured against Nixon's shoulder, steeling herself for the moment he got up to go home.

His hand was making lazy circles over her back. 'Think Rosie will make it without imploding?'

'She will, I mightn't. If I hear "how many more sleeps?" once more I'll scream.'

'I'll miss you two while I'm in Dunedin.' His hand pressed a little harder. 'I could stay here instead.'

'No, you've got to see your family.' He hadn't been dancing with excitement when he'd told her he was going to Dunedin for Christmas. More like apprehensive. 'I couldn't imagine not spending the day with Mum and Dad and the annoying brothers. It wouldn't be Christmas.'

'Your family is so together. Everyone loves each other so easily, comfortably.'

'You missed out there.'

'Once I'd have agreed.' He bit his lip. 'But I might be wrong.' A pause. 'Hate to admit this but I'm looking forward to spending time with everyone, seeing how the kids have grown. Getting to know Rosie has made me realise how much I've missed out on.'

'Could be your best Christmas ever.'

'Yeah.' A soft kiss on her brow before he told her, 'I'm back on duty on the twenty-seventh.'

Two days and nights without seeing Nixon. A lifetime. 'Glad you're having dinner with us tomorrow night before you hit the road south.' They'd agreed to get together with

Rosie for presents and an early meal, then she'd head out to the Valley to join her family.

Nixon's hand left her skin, and the bed rocked. 'Time I headed home.'

She wasn't ready to have Rosie bouncing into her bedroom in the morning to find Nixon in bed with her. Not when they hadn't talked about where they were going with this, while they were still in the exciting, don't-get-too-serious phase. To introduce Rosie to the possibility of Nixon staying in her life before she and Nixon had made that commitment would be plain irresponsible.

Rosie's heart would be broken. Already she thought he was the best thing after chocolate Santas. So did her mother. 'Ever thought of coating yourself in chocolate?'

Nixon's head jerked up. 'What? You want to lick it off me, by any chance?'

'Now there's a thought.'

'I'm not going to ask where you're going with this one.' He slid into his chinos and shoved his arms into his crumpled shirt before bending over to kiss her chin, her nose, and then finally her mouth. 'See you later.'

'I'll hold you to that.' She wasn't working again until after Christmas, having booked the days off long ago. Having worked half shifts most of the month, she and Nixon had agreed she'd return to work full time on the twenty-seventh.

Another kiss caressed her lips, and she snatched a handful of shirt, tugged him closer. 'What's the time?'

'Unfortunately I do need some shut-eye before returning to the ED.'

'Damn.' She craved another round of lovemaking.

'See you.' Emma sighed as the front door closed quietly. Bring on the time when he did stay right through until morning.

*Don't rush things.*

Nixon wasn't ready for anything serious, and she probably wasn't either. Memories of bad times returned at inconvenient moments, coming more frequently these past weeks, as though the more she got to know Nixon and thought he might be the man for her, the more her mind reminded her how wrong love could go.

Picking up the adjacent pillow, she buried her face in it to inhale deeply, savouring Nixon's scent. They were a work in progress, which was currently giving her unbelievable pleasure.

Forget moving ahead. She was already there, wherever that was. Right or wrong, she'd fallen in love with Nixon. Totally. Helplessly—which was the scare factor. She understood being helpless as only those who'd been in her situation did. But while caution tripped through the excitement, deep inside where it mattered she knew Nixon didn't have a violent bone in his body. He'd protect those he loved to the end of the earth. If only he could admit that love.

Nixon had given her back so much she felt like the optimistic girl she'd been before she married. And she gave him plenty of passion, warmth, fun, and genuine care. Another yawn had her putting the pillow aside and snuggling under the covers, her eyes drooping shut. Better buy some vitamins in the morning.

'Mummy, it's a robot.' Rosie tore at the paper left on the box Nixon had given her.

'Careful, my girl. You don't want to break it.' Emma smiled at Rosie's excitement. 'We've only just started. There's all tomorrow to get through yet.' Her smile slipped. She'd miss Nixon so much. Too much. It was only for two days—and nights. She rubbed her eyes with her thumbs. Her head pounded, and her breasts ached for the first time in days.

Nixon nodded. No easy smiles from him this afternoon.

'You okay?' she asked, trying not to let the grizzly mood that had been gnawing at her all day come to the fore.

'Busy day.' He concentrated too hard on opening the well-sealed box holding the robot.

Not what she wanted. She'd been looking forward to a few hours relaxing with Nixon over a wine as Rosie opened her present and he taught her how to operate the controls. So they were both in moods. Maybe this time of the year did that to him, reminded him of missing out with his parents and brother.

'Abbie came in for coffee and cake earlier. She's on a high about Christmas with her baby and how everything's going so well with Callum.' She hadn't shut up for a moment and Emma had felt drained when she'd picked up Grace and left. Not that she could blame her friend for feeling out of sorts. Hell, she didn't know what to blame it on, but if she had to pick a culprit she'd go with hormones. Always a good backstop.

'Hold the controls like this,' Nixon demonstrated to Rosie. 'Push that button.'

The robotic super girl lurched and fell over. 'I did it, Mummy. Look.'

Nixon stood the toy up again, and again, so patient. If she didn't know better she would have said he was an old hand at playing with kids. 'What time do you want to get away?'

He glanced up. 'Being Christmas Eve, the road will be chaotic, so about seven if that works for you.'

A couple of hours earlier than she'd expected, or believed from his comments when she'd first suggested dinner. 'I'll start cooking.' The salad was prepared, the peas podded, the spuds ready to be brought to the boil. She stood up in a hurry and tripped over a doll lying on the floor.

Nixon caught her as she reached out for balance and came to his feet. 'Steady.'

Emma breathed in Nixon's scent and felt tension in his hands. Something was wrong. Making eye contact with him, she saw worry and uncertainty coming back at her. 'What's up?'

'Nothing.'

Through the wall, Grace started crying, a loud, heart-string-tugging sound, and Emma's breasts tightened, her heart dropped, and a waterfall streamed from her eyes. Nothing, he'd said. It was just all too much. She fell against Nixon, wrapped her arms around his waist and cried, deep harsh sobs filled with sadness and longing and envy.

Nixon lifted her into his arms and sank onto a chair, holding her against his chest, his hand soothing her back, his lips brushing the top of her head. 'Rosie, take the robot to show Abbie, will you? I'll come and get you in a minute.'

'Can I?'

'Off you go.' A moment later he was pressing tissues from the box nearby into her hand. 'Hey, about time this happened.'

'This isn't baby hormones.' Emma sniffed. 'Not Grace ones.'

Under her backside he tensed. 'What do you mean?'

Because it had been a day full of yearning, feeling as though she was missing out and not knowing how to cope or where to find the strength to look life in the eye and tell it to go to hell, she opened her mouth and spilled. 'I want another baby. One of my own. Don't even think of telling me this is because of Grace. It's not.'

Nixon's chin rested on the top of her head. 'You're exhausted, Em. You've been rushing around pretending all is well in your court, that you're coping. Hell, you've avoided meetings with the counsellor, saying you don't need to download your heart. Give yourself a break.'

Pulling her face away from his sodden shirt, she stared at him. 'I know all that. You're still wrong. Not that it matters. Pregnancy's out when I'm not in a permanent, loving relationship.' What would he do if she told him her half of that picture existed? She loved Nixon, wanted him to be the father of her next child, but she'd gone off half cocked, hadn't waited until he was ready to hear what she was thinking. 'I'm sorry,' she blustered, afraid she'd scared him off for ever. 'You're right. I'm tired.' She sat up straighter, wiped her eyes and cheeks; his finger brushed her hair. 'Here's me being a cry baby and it's Christmas.'

Brushing her forehead with his lips, he gave her a lopsided smile. 'How about we skip dinner and you head out to your folks' while you're still awake? I can grab something from the supermarket as I go through Frankton.'

If her heart hadn't already felt like a lump of concrete that would've done it. He was bolting. Using her as the reason, but he hadn't been forthcoming with her since arriving, and now he was in a hurry to be gone. 'If that's what you want,' she said pointedly.

'It's best.' He stared at her with something she'd like to believe was love in his eyes, but her head screamed out that she knew better. She'd fallen for him, but doubted he felt the same. Pushing her case would be rushing him.

Clambering to her feet, she stared out of the window, seeing her hopes vaporising in the hot summer air. When Nixon draped an arm over her shoulders she couldn't help but lean into him, absorb his strength and heat. And hope against hope that time would bring her what she wanted.

'Merry Christmas, Nixon.'

# CHAPTER TWELVE

EMMA GRINNED. A WIDE, excited grin that tightened his gut with apprehension. 'Hey, Nixon, we're having a baby. How awesome is that?' She was grinning and dancing around ED as if she'd won the lottery. To her she probably had.

Not to him. He didn't need a lottery of any sort. 'A b-baby?' Nixon stuttered. 'Really?' Not true. She was teasing. He watched her, and heat filled his veins. He wanted her. Despite her bombshell he wanted to get close and hold her lithe body against his, to make love slowly and tenderly. To look into her eyes as she came and fall into the depths of their togetherness. She couldn't be pregnant. Not when they hadn't discussed this or anything about their future.

Now Emma moved closer and closer, her hands rubbing her stomach—her swollen, pregnant stomach. Those small hands spread across the taut cloth of her scrubs, gently holding her belly. 'Hey, put your hand on here,' she whispered. 'You can feel him kicking.'

Nixon stepped back, his butt coming up against the desk. 'You've had a test?'

Her eyes rolled. 'Do you think we need one?'

He thought they were not having a baby between them. Not yet. Probably never. He wasn't ready to be a dad.

Clapping filled the department, banged in his ears, slammed around his skull.

'It's good, isn't it?' Emma persisted.

Nixon shot up on the couch, sweat covering his skin, his heart pounding so hard his ribs were about to snap. The sheet was tangled around his feet, his pillow on the floor.

'Santa's been,' shouted Thomas. 'Get up, Uncle Nixon. We've got presents.'

Nixon gulped and stared at the two boys in their pyjamas and dragging laden pillowcases through the room. What the hell? He was in his cousin's lounge. There was a Christmas tree in the corner. Voices were coming from down the hall. His watch said five-ten. The sun was barely up.

'Look what we found on our beds, Uncle Nixon.' Mathew brought his goodies over to be inspected.

Nixon's feet hit the floor and he pushed himself to standing. He needed out of here, fresh air and solitude: not excited kids with their Christmas bounty. Emma and a baby? It was a bloody dream. Dream? Nightmare more like. He shivered despite the early sunlight coming through the windows. 'Em?' he croaked. It was a dream, man. Yeah, but what he wouldn't do to have her wrap her arms around him and say it was only a stupid nightmare.

'Some tea wouldn't go amiss about now.' Henry strolled into the room looking unfazed at the early hour.

'Be right with you,' Nixon managed as he pushed past to go to the bathroom, where he snapped the shower on and stood under an icy blast of water. Tried to blot out the image of Emma's hands gliding over her belly. Over their baby. It had been a nightmare. It would fade. He could not ruin Christmas day thinking about what it meant. His life had been turning around; he'd been so happy being with Emma and her girl. But a baby? Not this side of the next century. That was going too far. He wouldn't know how to cope, how to love the child, how to be the parent he'd missed and wanted all his life.

The shower didn't work. The dream remained at the forefront of his mind.

Watching the boys unwrapping presents and squealing with excitement pushed Emma aside briefly, but she returned the moment the family sat down for brunch. The laughter and chatter, the mountain of delicious food, champagne—his family. Despite the dream, he accepted their warmth and involvement with him. The kids were great, and he was getting to know them better. But one of his own? He had not moved that far forward.

*It wasn't for real.*

The dream was a warning to go slowly, be careful. A reminder of how life went belly up when he stepped outside his parameters.

His phone rang. Emma. He couldn't talk to her right now. He didn't know what to say, doubted he could talk without fear clogging his throat. Fear of losing her. Fear of having it all: Emma, Rosie, a home, more kids. He wasn't going there. He was the wrong man for her. He was a mess.

The ringing stopped, was quickly followed by a text. 'Call us when you're free.'

Next Christmas?

Nearly two hours later Nixon stared at the excited scene on his screen. 'I see the puppy's a hit.'

Em laughed softly. 'Rosie hasn't let her out of sight all morning.'

'Nixon, have you seen Bella? She's gorgeous. I love her. Mummy says I have to teach her about going to the toilet outside.'

'That'll be interesting,' he quipped around a huge lump blocking his windpipe. If only he could be with Emma today. And Rosie. If only he hadn't had that dream and didn't feel a deep trepidation. He'd had a wake-up call, could no longer continue seeing Emma if he felt so stressed over the thought of having children. He glanced at the woman inadvertently causing him anguish. 'How're you feeling today?'

Em's smile appeared forced. 'Great. Had a massive breakfast as only Mum knows how to make. She's already busy in the kitchen working on Christmas dinner. I'd help but turns out Daniel's girlfriend loves cooking so I got shunted out, told to put my feet up. How about you? Having a good time with your family?'

Yesterday's dark shadows under her eyes hadn't disappeared overnight. Say what she liked, she hadn't fully recovered yet. 'We were woken just after five by two lads who'd discovered Santa's presents on their beds, and nothing quietened down until a few minutes ago when everyone except Henry disappeared to the beach with some of the toys.'

Emma's soft laughter warmed him when he needed to be strong and stepping aside. 'You're glad you're with them?' she asked.

'Yes, I am.' The loud, loving greeting from everyone when he'd walked in the door of his cousin's house last night had stunned him. His family cared about him, had probably always loved him. Today, when he wasn't denying Emma and what they could have together if he could deal with the gremlins, he'd begun giving it back, cautiously sure, but he was stepping into new territory—and enjoying it.

'Nixon, look what my puppy does.' No peace when Rosie was around.

The dog was licking Rosie's face. 'Yukky.' He chuckled, happy to be a part of this child's life. At the moment. For how long was up to him and Emma. Once he'd worked his way through all his hang-ups. If he got through them.

'Here comes the gang,' Emma warned. 'Hope you're wearing your armour.'

The screen was taken over by her family, full of good cheer and a load of cheeky questions. By the time he hit 'end' Nixon felt as tired as Emma looked. Her family were full on—just like his, he realised. He'd noticed the easy care and love in her family before he had in his. They'd got him thinking about his past in ways he'd never considered before. They? Or Emma? Definitely Emma. She was becoming special. Becoming? Emma was the most important person in his life. Did he love her? Was it possible? Why not? She was beautiful, loyal, strong, generous to a fault. What wasn't to love about her?

'They sound like a great bunch.' Henry handed him a coffee. 'Emma someone special?'

Had he been listening to the whole conversation? Avoiding the loaded question, Nixon sipped the coffee and went with one of his own. 'Did I shut down immediately that day? Or did it take some time?' Then he clarified. 'We've never talked about it. Neither of us like talking about the deep and personal, but lately I find I need to know what makes me tick.'

'You withdrew the moment you were told about the accident.' Henry studied him for a long time. 'I've been waiting for this day for a long time. Sorry, lad, I should've found a way to bring it up but...' he shrugged '... I'm the one who never talks about our losses and unfortunately you learnt from me. Not the best role model you could've had.'

'I could've done a lot worse.' Nixon took another mouthful of coffee. Strong but not hitting the places that needed it. 'Any of that champagne left over from brunch?'

'Help yourself, and pour me one while you're at it.' Henry sat down at the outdoor table and stared out over the lawn.

Nixon was in charge of roasting the turkey so he poked the massive bird with a fork, adjusted the oven temperature and took two full glasses outside.

They sat relaxed in each other's company. Nixon couldn't remember a time when he'd done this before. His visits were usually focused, busy and followed a standard formula. Check how everyone was, see that Henry didn't need anything, have a meal to celebrate whatever occasion had brought him here, and then head away relieved it was over until the next time. This time he'd come for two nights, not the usual one, and for once he had no desire to hit the road back to Queenstown in a hurry.

Yet he did because Emma was there. Despite his fright over a baby he still wanted to see her, hold that sensational body and breathe her in, listen to her happy voice. She hadn't been happy yesterday. Downright sad because of Grace not being hers. She'd have loved the dream. His gut twisted tight. Dream for her, nightmare for him. Hopefully after a good night's sleep Emma realised her hormones had been at play, nothing else. This morning that sadness still lingered, so who knew what she felt about babies today? As much as he couldn't wait to see her, the brakes were clamping down on his feelings, making him hesitate. He wanted her in all facets of his life. And at the same time, he didn't. What if he didn't love her enough and hurt her accidentally? What if he did love her enough and got hurt himself?

'Don't make the same mistakes I did,' Henry intoned. Talking about himself would be as normal as a worm flying past.

Nixon didn't move a muscle, afraid he'd distract his uncle and that'd be the end of this odd conversation. Just because Henry had admitted to being closed, didn't mean he intended talking about everything from the past.

'Being older, my kids knew me way better than you and didn't let me get away with a thing. But it was easy to stay aloof from you. You shut down, held in all the pain, the fear, the uncertainty. I knew what was going on in your head.'

'I've finally worked that out.' Now he could see it was so obvious. No hugs, no talks about his family. But he'd been cared for, safe, fed and clothed. 'You lost your wife, and then your sister.'

'It was a bad time.' Henry drained his glass.

Nixon went to refill it. It was Christmas morning after all and they were having quite the conversation. Damn it. He took the bottle outside. 'Tell me about Mum. I remember her always laughing, and she sang a lot.'

'You call that singing? Haven't I taught you anything?' Henry chuckled. 'But, yes, she loved to sing. But most of all she loved her boys. You were everything to her. You two and your father. I'd never known her to be so happy.'

Nixon sipped his wine, absorbing this knowledge. 'Thank you.'

Out on the street some youngsters played, shouting and laughing, reminding him of Rosie. Such a well-rounded girl because she had a wonderful, caring, fiercely protective mother. Emma didn't have any problems letting him get close to her daughter, to taking part in small ways in her life. Had Emma let her guard down? Was he worthy of her trust?

'Don't make the same mistakes I did.' There was a ton of regret in Henry's voice. 'I could've remarried, had another chance at happiness but I refused to let her in.'

'It's not too late.'

Henry sipped his drink. 'No, lad, it's not.'

'Doing anything exciting tonight?' Steph asked Emma as they headed into ED a week later.

It was New Year's Eve and Queenstown would be party central. 'Staying out at the Valley. Mum and Dad always have open house.' Emma laughed. 'Rosie and I have been there since Christmas.' The three days she'd been at work had been busy, and she was looking forward to the New Year public holidays for some rest. When would she start to feel normal again? This tiredness had gone on too long.

'How's that puppy coping with Rosie?' Nixon called from his office as she passed.

Emma's heart fluttered. She'd missed him. His uncle had taken ill on Boxing Day and Nixon had remained in Dunedin until last night, making sure Henry rested. They'd talked every day but it wasn't the same as being with him. There'd been a hesitation in his voice she couldn't pinpoint. Stepping inside the office, she told him, 'They're inseparable. How's Henry?' Damn but he was beautiful. That lean body and those tight muscles at the edges of his scrubs' sleeves. That mouth that did amazing things to her body.

'Back to his usual taciturn self,' Nixon replied fondly, which was unusual. He was normally guarded when talking about his family. How likely was it that they'd talked about the past and whatever held Nixon back?

Walking around the desk, she leaned in to kiss him, inhaled him, felt his shoulders under her hands. 'I missed you. You still game for tonight?' She'd invited him to join her at her family's home for the night. As in, stay over in the spare bedroom, and hopefully sneak down the hall to her room like two naughty teens when the lights went out.

Pewter eyes met hers, clear of any hesitation now. 'You bet.'

'Good answer.' She'd held lingering doubts that he was going to continue seeing her when he returned. That meltdown she'd had on Christmas Eve had rattled him as much as her, though for different reasons. Shock had marred his face when she'd said she wanted a baby. As well it might. They weren't anywhere near ready for that level of commitment. Nor was she ready to carry another baby. She had to wait, enjoy being with Nixon and slowly bring him around to seeing he could have a loving life with her and Rosie. If he wanted to…and she thought he might.

Nixon cupped her head to draw her close again.

'Hmm,' Steph cleared her throat. 'Nixon, you're needed in Resus.'

'Right.' He was up and moving towards the door. 'Nothing like reality to remind me where we are.'

Following him, Emma envied the energy blasting off him as those long legs ate up the distance to Resus. Right on cue a yawn stretched her mouth.

'You're still doing that?' Nixon asked as he reached for the patient notes being held out to him. But then he was reading and she ducked out of answering.

Until the middle of shift when he caught her out again. 'Think you need your iron levels checked? The pregnancy could've caused anaemia.'

'My haemoglobin is around one twenty.' Not anaemic by any stretch.

'Let's get it checked anyway.' Nixon took her elbow and led her to his office. 'I'll fill out a lab request so you can get it done before you leave work.'

With Nixon acting on her exhaustion she felt worse. This tiredness was for real, not something her imagination had conjured up. 'Okay.'

Nixon printed a request form and signed it with a flourish. 'Don't put it off.'

'I said okay,' she snapped, letting the tiredness get to her. Instead of gaining more energy, her body was on a downhill slide and even her boobs had returned to aching at inconvenient moments.

'Go now while we're not busy.'

'Thanks.' She'd be a load of fun tonight like this. The lift was waiting, as though expecting her. She hit the floor number and leaned back against the cool wall. Her boobs ached. As they had when her milk was drying up. Or when she was in the early stages of pregnancy with Grace.

Emma straightened up fast. 'No way. Can't be.'

Women didn't get pregnant this soon after giving birth. Huh? Which nursing textbook did she get that out of? Just as breastfeeding didn't act as birth control, there was no downtime when sex was safe. But she and Nixon had been careful, always used condoms. Had to be low iron. Could not be any other reason.

It had been a month since Grace's arrival. No bloody way.

The lab form shook in her hand as she stared at the tests Nixon had requested. CBC and iron studies. Nothing startling, nothing to change the momentum of her life. Unless the CBC showed some abnormality with her white or red cells, or platelets, which hadn't occurred to either her or Nixon. But nor had that idea her brain had just thrown at her. Had they used a condom each and every time they'd made love? Yes, she'd swear they had.

The lift shook to a stop on the floor holding the lab. Emma shivered. Stepping through the door, she hesitated, wanted to run, head home to hide under the bedcovers. Go to sleep and wake up knowing she'd been silly even to consider she might be pregnant. Glancing down the hall, she saw Cindy, a pal from school who'd played goal shoot to her goal defence when she played netball in winter. If ever she needed Cindy, now was it.

'Hello, what brings you up here?' asked Cindy the moment she saw Emma.

'I need a blood test.' She shoved the form into Cindy's hand. 'I know it's not your job but can you take the specimen? I need to ask you something.' Lab technicians were trained to take blood samples.

'Come with me.' Cindy led her into a little used cubicle. 'Sit and tell me what's got you in a sweat.'

'You're working in biochemistry, right?' When Cindy nodded, she continued. 'Is there any chance you could run an HCG for me? I'll make it legit by paying, but I don't want the result going to the doctor who signed the form.'

Cindy's eyes widened, but all she said was, 'Sure.'

Within minutes Emma was on her way back to the department, the worry that had been gnawing at her for hours put to rest. It was as though, now she'd faced the real possibility she could be pregnant, she wasn't bothered. The panic had gone. Only to return if the HCG test showed positive.

Then she'd have to face reality and make some difficult decisions.

She'd have to think of Rosie, and her family.

Her job. How could she continue to work if she had a baby as well as a school-age child?

She'd have to confront Nixon.

Panic flared, returned harder and tighter than the first round. Emma backed up against the wall, out of the way of patients and staff, working at keeping herself from doing a face plant as her knees no longer had the strength to hold her upright.

'How long do you intend holding up that wall?' came the deep, sexy voice of the man who would be propping up the wall himself if he knew.

The test would come back negative. She'd take some iron tablets and be back to normal in no time at all. It came down to the fact she'd worked throughout her pregnancy and gone back to work only days after the birth. She aimed for casual and confident, even though she must look like someone who'd camped out all week under a bridge. 'As long as it needs me.'

A firm hand on her elbow lifted her away from that helpful wall. 'You're starting to worry me.'

*I'm worrying myself.*

'Should have the answers to the tests within an hour.' *Click, click.* One vertebra at a time she drew herself up as tall as possible, but still short beside this man. That was one of the things she adored about him. He made her feel tiny and safe against his length and strength.

'We need to talk. If you're seriously unwell I'd like to know. No, damn it, I need to know. No argument.' Nixon looking out for her was awesome, and heartening. Make that heart-stopping.

*Don't let me be pregnant.*

That'd knock him back into I-am-only-a-friend-with-no-involvement. Even though he seemed different, that attitude still lurked on the periphery, ready to pounce. 'Let's get back to patients.' The focus on her was disturbing. What if they'd made a baby?

They had.

Emma sank to her haunches and stared at the phone in her hand as though it were a monster. Her head swirled with the connotations of her predicament. A baby. How careless was that? She'd started thinking another child would be wonderful, but that picture had a father for the baby in it, a caring parent for Rosie, a loving partner for her.

*Careful what you wish for.*

Now she got that message in black and white. No grey areas. Nixon would put his hand up, yes. Be a responsible man, yes. Give her his heart, doubtful. *A grey area.* Her head hurt.

It was New Year's Eve, the night she was taking Nixon home to her family as a partner, as someone she loved and wanted them to get to know a whole lot better.

'Em? What's wrong?'

Her worst nightmare had found her in the drugs room. No, that was unfair. Nixon was not a nightmare. He was a loving man she'd given her heart to and now she had to drop a bomb in his hand. She took the hand he held out to her and dragged herself upright.

*Tell him. Not now. We're at work. Coward. Nothing's going to change the longer you leave telling him. You'll only make it harder on yourself.*

But keeping Nixon in oblivion for a little while longer would give him a few more hours' peace.

Then she looked at him, found his worried gaze searching her face for answers, and knew she was being selfish. 'I'm pregnant.'

'We are?' Shock and disbelief warred across his face.

*We* are. That gave her hope. He hadn't disappeared down the corridor and locked himself in his office. Yet. She nodded, incapable of forming words.

'That's why you're so tired. I should've guessed.' He shoved a hand through his hair. 'Your iron and haemoglobin all normal?'

Again she nodded.

'I think I knew they would be. I feel as though a cloud has lifted from something I've been denying.' When she stared at him he rattled her with, 'I think I might've known deep down.'

Finally her larynx started working. 'We were always careful.'

One dark eyebrow rose in irony. 'Must've got a dud. Doesn't matter how it happened, the fact is it did. How are you feeling about this?'

How are *you* feeling? 'It's still sinking in.' Cop out, but true. 'I know I'll have it and keep it. Even if that makes me look like a careless slut.'

'Don't insult yourself. Or me.' His fingers brushed her cheek, took her chin gently and lifted her head so she had to look into his eyes. 'We need time to absorb what this means to all of us.'

He still wasn't running. It felt too good to be true. This man didn't get involved. Emma shivered and stepped away from those gentle fingers. She needed answers now, not tomorrow or in the new year. She wasn't going to get them. Nixon needed space. She needed reassurance. The only person in this picture who was going to give her that right now was herself. 'Here's the thing. I already know what it means. Been here before, remember?' She didn't give him time to reply. 'Only this time it's different. This time I want the father in the picture. I want a family: you, me, Rosie and the baby.'

He took a step back, cracking her heart in the process. No surprise there.

'I've fallen in love with you, Nixon. I didn't mean to, I knew you'd probably never feel the same way about me, but it's happened and I can't undo it.' The truth sucked big time, but if she didn't put it out there she wasn't going in to bat for her baby. Or herself.

Nixon took another backward step, and the cracks widened.

'I love you.' It was surprising how easy it was to say. It was true, and right, and, hell, it was killing her on the inside. She stared at him, willing him to answer, to put her heart at ease. The silence was laden, heavy and chilly. Finally, she said, 'Time I got back to work.' She needed to get a grip or she'd be a danger to any patient who came near her.

'Take the rest of the day off, Emma.'

'It's all right.'

'No, it's not. You've had a shock.' He was ignoring the love factor. Wouldn't know how to digest that news. 'Go home, put your feet up.'

'You want me out of the way. Out of sight, off the radar, so I'm not reminding you every minute about the problem lying between us.'

'We need space while we get our heads around this. Don't you agree?'

'Not for a moment. I'm not skulking off when we're busy so *you* can avoid *me*.'

'Give me time, Emma. That's all I ask.'

'Yeah, and there lies the problem. You want time, not a baby or me or involvement.' Crikey, she had grown a backbone after all. Or was she being harsh? 'Sorry.' A yawn followed.

'Go home, Em. For your sake, not mine.'

Her bed beckoned, the quiet, the solitude; Abbie banging down the door to ask why she was home. 'No can do. I have a job to do and I'm going to do it. I don't run at the first sign of trouble.'

His nod was curt. 'I think I'll take a rain check on tonight with your family though.'

She might've seen that coming but it still hurt like stink. 'Avoid me as much as you like but we are involved now. There's nothing you can do to change that.'

Pain filled his gaze, tightened his face, then was gone, leaving—despair. He turned away.

Her heart thumped hard, for him, for her. 'Nixon?'

He turned slowly, one eyebrow elevated. 'Emma.'

The chill in her name froze her to the spot. Backbone remember? Swallow. 'I could've gift-wrapped the news, but we both believe in plain truth. I am pregnant, and I do love you. There's no hidden catch.'

'I didn't think there was.' He stalked away, disappeared into Resus, leaving her alone and frightened.

She'd fallen for a man who couldn't find it in him to admit to love. They were having a baby and he had no idea how to deal with it. Which left her stranded, in need of him, of his love.

'Emma, can you take the fractured femur arriving in

two?' Steph stepped into her line of vision. 'Are you all right? You're not coming down with the stomach virus too?'

*Suck it up, get on with life as you knew it before Nixon stole your heart.* 'I'm good. Who's our patient? Local or tourist?' She got busy, burying herself in other people's problems and pain, ignoring her own, barely coming up for air, ignoring Nixon, until shift ended. At four o'clock she drove up her parents' driveway, walked inside and burst into tears the moment her mother looked at her.

Happy new year.

Nixon pedalled as if his life depended on it. Arrowtown had never appeared on the horizon so quickly, and he hadn't finished thinking through what he was going to do. He'd barely started. Focusing entirely on riding hard and safe was easier than the fear and trepidation kicking up a storm in his belly.

A baby. He was going to be a father. Nightmares did come true.

The township was quiet, the tourists gone for the day. Nixon wheeled along the streets, barely noticing his surrounds. Emma was pregnant with his baby. He got that in spades. But knowing, and then knowing what to do—different pages, different books.

A cat streaked across the road in front of him. Braking hard, he fought to remain upright and on the tarmac. Blasted animal. A broken collarbone wouldn't help anything. Heading for the park at the end of the main street, Nixon dropped his bike on the grass and sank his butt onto a picnic table.

The sun was dropping behind the hills but that wasn't why he was shivering.

Emma was carrying his baby. He was going to be a dad. Like it or not. Too late for choosing whether to chance becoming a parent. Too late to heed the warning from his nightmare. It was a done deal. Not that he wished the baby away. No, excitement stirred his blood, then reality kicked in and fear engulfed him. He knew little about loving someone. He wanted Emma. In his life. In his heart. Everywhere, all the time. If only he knew how. It should be as easy as sitting down and talking with her, explaining himself—if laying his heart on the line were his way. It wasn't.

Em had knocked his socks off saying she loved him. Her declaration had turned him hot and cold all at once. He wanted her love, needed to show her he loved her, but a lifetime of holding back was in the way. There were no guidelines. Anyway, it probably wasn't even possible.

'I love you.' Emma's words resonated endlessly, had kept him on edge for the rest of shift. Every time he'd seen her he'd wanted to rush over and shake some sense into her head, make her see he was the wrong man to be looking at a future with. 'We're having a baby.'

Riding was supposed to settle his head, but his heart wasn't in it. He was running away. He and Emma were having a baby. She'd been stoic when he'd said he wasn't going to her family dinner, not showing relief or disappointment. Which had rubbed him up the wrong way. He'd wanted a reaction, something to guide him through this murky situation. But no. She'd left him to make up his own mind—about everything.

'Don't make the same mistakes I did.'

*Sure, thanks, Henry. I'll keep that in mind.*

The man who'd talked to him last week for the first time. The man who'd taken his real father's place as best he could. Should he ask his advice? No, this decision was his alone. But no harm in getting some input. Digging his phone out of his cycle pants, he pressed a number. 'Henry, it's me.'

'I'm sixty-five, not ninety-five. My phone is state of the art.'

'Of course.' Nixon had given it to him for his last birthday.

'What's up?' Straight to the point.

Hang up or tell Henry? Flight or fight? Gulp. 'I don't know what to do. I'm going to be a father.'

Henry was quiet, and Nixon could see the frown forming between his bushy eyebrows and the meditative look in his eyes. Then, 'This anything to do with Emma?'

'Yes.'

'You love her?'

*Go for the throat, why don't you?*

'I—' Swallow. 'Yes.'

'Does she know that?'

*You know she doesn't, you old bugger.*

'It's not so easy.'

Another silence, then, 'Yes, Nixon, it is. If you truly love her then you open your mouth and tell her.'

More silence. He had no answer to that gem. Because Henry was right. That was how people communicated. Most people. Just not him. 'I've never said those words to anyone in my life.' Not that he was telling Henry something he didn't know.

'Time you started. It's not that you don't know how to love.'

His eyes moistened, damn it. Henry was digging under his skin, scratching the painful scars. He didn't know how to say I love you. Did he just open his mouth and spill? Or did there need to be a lead in? Not an orchestra or roses; he got that. But to say those three words—once they were out, there was no taking them back to protect his heart. He'd be vulnerable. Emma mightn't walk away from him but she could get injured, die. The other day she'd been so exhausted it had crippled her. What if it had been worse?

Something other than pregnancy doing that to her? He'd have lost his heart, the woman he loved. Or equally bad: what if he failed her? Found his love wasn't strong and true? No, he was sure about that.

Scrubbing a hand across his eyes, he coughed. Henry was waiting patiently. Damn but he owed this man. 'Henry—'

'It's all right. Go and tell this special woman how you feel. Then bring her down to meet us. If you're going to set up family we're going to be part of the picture. All of us.' Then he was gone.

It was that easy? Yeah, sure. Nixon began riding back to Queenstown, taking a different route, riding slower as he let Henry's advice wash over him, into him.

Tell her.

Family. Emma. Children. A home. A baby.

He passed a real-estate sign with a photo showing a large family home set in paddocks. The house that had been advertised in the paper before Christmas. The house Emma thought would be perfect for her and Rosie and anyone else she might love.

His speed fell away as he stared over the fence at the house coming into view from behind a row of birch trees. Placing his feet on the ground, he took in the wide verandas, the bay windows, two chimneys, the rose-filled gardens. Yes, Emma could be happy there. But this had nothing to do with them and their current situation. This house was not going to tell Emma he loved her.

Or was it? What if he showed Emma how much he loved her? He could do that. He could. Words weren't the only way of putting his feelings out there. His heart pumped faster, harder, and the need to act expanded through his chest, became urgent. If he couldn't do this for Emma he didn't deserve her. Then what would his life be like? Empty. Lonely. Unbearable.

* * *

Emma looked up from the bacon she was cutting into ever smaller pieces on her plate. 'Expecting someone for breakfast?' she asked her father. The house was quiet the next morning as most people slept off last night's party.

'Nope. Sure you didn't invite a certain someone?' Her father winked as he glanced out of the window.

'What?'

Rosie was racing for the door, Bella at her heels. 'Nixon!'

'What does this mean?' Emma whispered, trying to ignore the hope thrashing against her heart. Good? Or bad? Were they getting together, or was it over before it got started?

'Why don't you go and find out, love?' Her father patted her hand.

Nixon had been blunt about wanting time to himself yesterday. Every time a car had come up the drive last night her heart had lifted in hope, and dived back down when it hadn't been Nixon. She hadn't slept a wink all night for fear he'd reject her. Was that why he was here now? To tell her he couldn't be the man she wanted? Or—

Her legs refused to lift her up. Remaining seated, shaking on the inside, she refused to acknowledge the fledgling hope firing in her gut. This could all be the biggest let-down of her life.

Then Nixon was standing at the end of the table, Rosie's hand wrapped in his. 'Sorry to barge in like this, but I need to talk to Emma.'

She tried pushing up from the table; again her legs failed her. At least her neck muscles worked and she could meet his steady gaze. A lot steadier than her heart.

Her father held his hand out. 'Come on, Rosie. We'll take Bella to the pond.'

They both watched them leave as though that were the most important issue right now. The air stalled in Emma's lungs. 'Do you want some coffee?' she finally asked to fill in the tight silence.

'I'll get it.' He stepped across to the table and picked up a mug. Coffee splashed on the tablecloth when he poured.

Finally she couldn't stand it any longer. 'Tell me.'

He looked at her for a long moment, an emotion she couldn't identify in his eyes. 'I'm sorry about yesterday. It was a shock and I didn't handle it well.'

'You needed time to get your head around the baby.' He'd known almost as long as her.

'Not as much as what else you told me.' He hesitated.

Emma waited for her world to implode.

'I've struggled with putting my emotions out there since the day they told me my family was gone. I think I believed if I didn't say a word it wouldn't be true. Later I couldn't find the words, so I kept quiet. To my detriment. To your detriment.'

Hers? That had to mean something good. Didn't it? 'And?' She was rushing him. But, hell, how could she not? She wanted this over, no matter what he told her.

'I want us to have a future, Em.' More coffee splashed on the cloth and Nixon carefully placed the mug on the table. 'The four of us.'

She liked where this was going, but they were only at the beginning. 'As in, a family?'

'Yes.'

Her heart jerked, stabbing her painfully. 'Are you doing this for the baby's sake? Because you have a responsibility towards it? I can't accept that. It's all or nothing for me.' Where had the strength to say that come from? On the inside she was a bubbling mess of fear. Her mouth was a desert.

Nixon pulled some papers from his pocket. 'You'd better see this.'

A legal document. No way. She wasn't signing any

damned piece of paper that put the baby entirely in her custody. Or took it away from her. She stared at Nixon, saw the man she'd given her heart to, saw the strength, the honesty, the big heart, the fears and the care. He would not do that to her. Or his child. Reaching out, she asked, 'What is it?'

'Take a look.'

Slowly unfolding the document, she gasped. 'It's a sale and purchase agreement.' Quickly lowering her gaze, she read some more. 'Trish and Bill's place?'

'Yes.'

'I don't understand.'

'I looked around the property last night, and negotiated with the agent this morning. It's ours.'

Emma's butt was glued to her chair. 'Ours?' Did this mean…? She had no idea what it meant. Or rather, she was afraid to contemplate it in case she was wrong.

Nixon smiled that long, slow, heart-stopping smile of his as he moved closer. Reaching down, he pulled her up into his arms. 'Yes, ours. As in our home for our family. I know you love the property. I agree it is amazing, perfect really.'

'You're serious?' she squealed. Of course he would be. Nixon would never say so otherwise. 'We're going to live there?'

'You and me, and Rosie and the baby. And Bella.' He nodded. 'Yes, Em. That's what I mean.'

'But—' Her hands moved up his chest, up to his face. 'You want to live with me? As a family?'

'As your husband. Will you marry me?'

A hundred questions pushed forward as her smile started a slow widening and softening, turning up at the corners, lightening her heart. Nixon had proposed. That had to mean he loved her. Didn't it? The smile slowed, held position. 'This really isn't for the baby's sake?'

'No.' He looked up at the ceiling and puffed out a breath. 'Not at all. It's you I want to spend my life with. You and our family.'

Unbelievable words from Nixon. He'd come a long way. But he hadn't said he loved her. Not a dickey bird. Disappointment railed against elation. Nixon wanted to be with her for ever. It should be all she wanted. Call her greedy, but it wasn't enough. He'd buy her a house but not say those important three words. Even if only once. Once was enough. She'd cherish them, hold them close. But she had to hear them. Tipping back in his hold, she said, 'You bought this house because I said I loved it?'

The air quivered between them. 'Yes.'

'An impromptu decision?' Please say no.

'No.' Phew. 'And yes.'

Great. Now what? 'Can you elaborate?'

*Thump, thump*, went her heart.

*I know it's hard, but please, I need to know.*

'It happened very fast, but it feels right.' Nixon shoved his hands deep into the pockets of his chinos and strolled, oh, so deliberately, across to the bay window to stare out at Rosie playing in the pond. Then he turned to her. 'When Trish mentioned they were selling, this longing filled your eyes, a longing that got to me, made me wake up to the fact I wanted a part of that. Wanted it with you. You've got to me, Em. Under my skin, in my head, in…'

She took a step forward, said softly, 'Go on.'

'You're there all the time, even when you're someplace else.'

Another step. 'That's how it is for me too.' One more step.

'I want to be with you for the rest of my life. I want to marry you, Emma.'

'I want to marry you, Nixon. I love you,' she added as she reached him.

He looked away, swallowed, turned to face her, reached for her hands, held them as though they were fragile as spun sugar. 'You want me to tell you?'

She nodded. And waited.

Finally, 'I love you,' he whispered, a shiver in his fingers.

Up on her toes, reaching for his mouth with hers, her heart going crazy against her ribs, she kissed him. Long and deep and filled with love. Then she pulled back. 'Thank you. Yes, Nixon, I will marry you, because we love each other.' Then she went back to kissing him, knowing he couldn't say any more, he'd laid not just his heart but everything about him on the line by uttering those words. He'd shown her his love, he'd put it out there in actions—and in the best three words ever. 'I will never hurt you, Nixon.'

'I know.' Cocky right to the end now he'd got over the biggest hurdle of his life.

She grinned. 'So we've got ourselves a house, huh?'

'With lots of bedrooms for the family we're going to keep adding to.'

'You're getting carried away, my man.'

'My man, huh?' His kiss was full of promise and the future, and, yes, lots of love.

'Happy New Year,' she whispered against his mouth. What a way to start.

# EPILOGUE

*Next Christmas...*

'MUMMY, CAN I open Jack's presents from Santa? He's too little to do it,' Rosie pointed out earnestly, the excitement that had dragged them out of bed twenty minutes ago temporarily reined in while she waited for permission for her next adventure.

The stocking at the end of her bed hadn't taken very long to deal with and she was struggling with not being allowed to open any more presents until all the family arrived for brunch.

'When Dad's here you can.' Emma held baby Jack against her breast as she sat curled up in the leather rocker Nixon had bought her for nursing when he was born. It was her favourite go-to place inside the house, and this morning—yawn, it wasn't six o'clock yet—the decorated pine tree with the presents underneath filled her vision. Another Christmas. They seemed to come around awfully fast. But she didn't mind. There was always something wonderful happening at this time of year.

'Get this into you.' Nixon placed a mug of tea on the table at her elbow before dropping a kiss on the top of her head. 'Jack more interested in his breakfast?'

'Make the most of it. Next year will be different.' She

smiled up at this amazing man who'd stolen her heart and delivered his in a million ways ever since.

'Dad's here now. I can open Jack's stocking.'

'Bring it over to me and we'll do it together.' Nixon sipped his tea and dropped onto the floor beside Emma's rocker.

Rosie upended the stocking. 'What do you think Santa's got him, Dad?'

Emma's heart expanded with warmth. Dad. From the day she'd told Rosie Nixon wanted to adopt her and be her daddy she had never called him anything else. And Nixon had filled with pride and happiness and love.

Love. He still didn't say those three words very often. After the day he proposed she'd had to wait until their wedding day. Standing on their front lawn, surrounded by their families and friends, he had said, 'I love you, Emma Wright,' as he slid the wedding band onto her finger.

He'd said it again the day the adoption was finalised, and then when he held Jack in his arms for the first time.

Every time Nixon told her his face was filled with awe and love and everything she could ask for. It was enough. She didn't need to be told every day or even every week. Because he was constantly showing her. The cups of tea in bed first thing in the morning, the paintwork in the bathroom, the laundry hung out before he headed into work. Those kisses that melted her bones.

'Look, Jack. You've got a book like I had when I was little. It's made of really thick paper so you can't rip it.' Rosie reached for another parcel, squeezed and shook it. 'What's this?'

As though he knew he was missing out on something, Jack pulled his mouth away from breakfast and wriggled so he could see his sister. Emma cleaned his face and sat him up on her knee. 'There you go, wee man.'

'Go easy. You don't want to break it.' Nixon gently removed the parcel and laid it on the floor. 'Take the paper off slowly.'

'It's a caterpillar. A long one with funny pictures on its bumps.' Rosie leapt up and brought it over to Emma and Jack. 'See, Jack?'

'Careful.' Emma put a hand up between Jack's head and the toy, and when Rosie stepped back she reached for her tea. 'Right, guess we need to get dressed and ready for the influx.'

'No rush.' Nixon looked up at her. 'No one will be here for a couple of hours.'

'You're forgetting my family turn up when they're ready, not when we might be. Mum will be taking over the kitchen before you know it.' She was doing Christmas dinner here as Nixon's family were all driving up from Dunedin this morning.

Nixon just grinned. 'Rosie, can you bring me that red envelope with the big green bow on it, please?'

'Who's it for, Dad?' She placed it in Nixon's outstretched hand. 'Can I open it?'

'Not this one, my girl.' He stood up and lifted Jack into his arms before handing Emma the envelope. 'Merry Christmas, darling.' His eyes were filled with love and hope. Hope that he'd done the right thing?

Her heart fluttered. 'What is it?' she asked as she slid a finger under the back of the envelope and opened it. She tipped out the contents. Two photos. Of a beautiful black horse. Her head tipped up as she sought those wonderful grey eyes again. 'For me?' she whispered.

Nixon nodded. 'But you have to meet her first, see if you like her. If not we'll find another one.'

Emma leapt up and wrapped her arms around her husband. 'I love you so much. And not because you're buying me a horse, but because you're you. Wonderful, caring, kind…' Her throat filled up and happy tears streaked down her face. Crying had never really stopped since she'd had Grace, only this past year without exception they'd been happy tears.

'Carry on. I'm enjoying this,' Nixon murmured against her ear.

'And cheeky,' she managed.

His lips caressed hers. 'I love you, Emma.'

Wow. He'd said it again. That was a bigger present than any other he could give her.

'Merry Christmas.'

* * * * *

*Don't miss the first story in*
THE ULTIMATE CHRISTMAS GIFT *duet*
*THE NURSE'S SPECIAL DELIVERY*
*by Louisa George*

*And if you enjoyed this story*
*check out these other great reads*
*from Sue MacKay*

*FALLING FOR HER FAKE FIANCÉ*
*PREGNANT WITH THE BOSS'S BABY*
*RESISTING HER ARMY DOC RIVAL*
*THE ARMY DOC'S BABY BOMBSHELL*

*All available now!*

# WE'RE HAVING A MAKEOVER...

We'll still be bringing you the very best in romance from authors you love...all with a fabulous new look!

Look out for our stylish new logo, too

MILLS & BOON

COMING JANUARY 2018

# MILLS & BOON®

## *EXCLUSIVE EXTRACT*

One sizzling encounter with trauma doc Major Elle Caplin is all it takes to tempt Lieutenant Colonel Fitzwilliam to break his one-night rule…!

*Read on for a sneak preview of*
TEMPTED BY DR OFF-LIMITS
*the second book in Charlotte Hawkes's*
HOT ARMY DOCS *duet*

Fitz forgot everything. He simply indulged. For what seemed like an eternity, his mouth slid over hers. When he pushed, she pushed back. When he held back, Elle sought him. He trailed kisses down her jaw, her collarbone and to the hollow at the base of her neck. Her shivers of pleasure stoked his need. And each time he returned to those plump, pink lips, her mouth reached for his and her tongue met his in the same sinfully sinuous dance.

As he gave himself up to the sensations, as each kiss from Elle threatened to undermine every defence he'd spent years putting in place, the plink of those warm droplets on his ice-block heart growing more insistent.

Before he could help himself, he'd released the curtain of reds and golds from its military bun, inhaling its familiar fresh, floral scent as his hands buried themselves in its luxuriant depths. He could recall exactly how it had felt brushing over his naked skin that night and his body tightened.

'Gabrielle,' he groaned, unable to make up his mind whether it was a groan or a warning growl.

And still he kissed her, sometimes gently and reverently, other times hard and greedily. As though he never wanted to stop. He didn't know when he backed her up so that she was sitting on his desk with him standing between her legs, or when his fingers crept under the hem of her tee, or when he lifted it over her head and dropped it in a puddle on the plans he was supposed to be going through.

He needed to stop. Needed to remind her—remind himself—what kind of a man he was. How he would inevitably hurt her.